FLYING S

A Men of Londor

*From Canning Town to Royal Docks,
there's no escaping love.*

Susan Mac Nicol

The Men of London

Love You Senseless

Sight and Sinners

Suit Yourself

Feat of Clay

Cross to Bare

Flying Solo

Other Books By Susan Mac Nicol

Cassandra by Starlight

The Magick of Christmas

Confounding Cupid

Together in Starlight

Stripped Bare

Saving Alexander

Worth Keeping

Double Alchemy

Double Alchemy: Climax

Love and Punishment

Out for the Holidays

Boroughs
Publishing Group

www.BOROUGHSPUBLISHINGGROUP.com

FLYING SOLO
Copyright © 2016 Susan Elaine Mac Nicol

ISBN 978-1-523621-58-3

To those people with nowhere to go, the homeless of the world as they struggle to survive. We do see you; it's simply that sometimes we can't acknowledge you're there. To do so would mean feeling uncomfortable and having a conscience. We should all try harder to help you and make sure you can always be seen.

Also, to those who care about them, the charities and people who help without judgement: You are the true heroes. Never forget that you do make a difference, and for that we are all forever grateful.

ACKNOWLEDGMENTS

The character of Maxwell is loosely based on a friend of mine called Warren Joseph Allen. We've had some conversations I can't repeat here, because I'm a lady, and he's taught me a few things I really didn't need to know but enjoyed learning about all the same. He's sassy, a diva, but much like Maxwell in character—I believe, anyway. Thanks, Warren, for allowing me to use certain personal insights, quirks and habits in my story. I won't tell which ones are true, if you won't. :) Hint: He can be bribed to tell all for the price of a pair of Andrew Christians.

The game Gibson is designing is a bit of fun. *Camp Queen* sounded like a rollicking good game, though, and if anyone fancies developing it, let me know. It could be a lot of fun.

FLYING SOLO

Prologue

Snowflakes drifted past Mooch, peppering his already freezing face with pinpricks of icy spite. Huddled under his tattered blanket, he pulled his threadbare jersey and jacket tighter around his shuddering body. The shop doorway he and Levi sheltered in was scarce protection from the heavy flakes blanketing the dismal London streets.

In the corner, curled into a foetal ball, Levi slept, face under a bright red cover sprinkled with stark white. Mooch had recently returned from a bit of dumpster diving to find his street partner sleeping. Despite his ire at that fact—Levi was supposed to be watching their stuff—Mooch hadn't the heart to wake him. Sleep came grudgingly to Levi. Instead Mooch had checked they still had their meagre belongings and had given a sigh of relief when he confirmed they were intact.

As for food, he'd found nothing other than half a sandwich already green and mouldy and not worth eating. Mooch had standards and he wasn't prepared to risk another bout of gastroenteritis for himself or Levi.

He reached over and tucked the grimy blanket over Levi, making sure the hand out in the open was pushed back under the thin covering—a hand already blue and cold, its fingernails ragged and bitten and spattered with cuts and nicks.

Mooch was tired; the cold had invaded his body like a sly enemy trying to wear him down, trying to make him acquiesce to the demand he simply lie down and never wake up.

"Not going to happen," he muttered through chapped, torn lips. "Bitch is not going to get the better of me." He glanced over at Levi. "Not while he needs me anyway."

No matter how he'd tried to cajole Levi off drugs with sex, love and threats of leaving him, nothing made a difference. If Mooch thought it might help, he'd find Levi's dealers and punch their lights out, warn them to leave him alone. But Mooch knew, as soon as one went down, another low life sprung up in their place. At least Levi had one woman he trusted who was better than a stranger. It was safer for him that way.

A passer-by glanced at them, a faint look of disgust on his face. Mooch sneered, willing the stranger to pass so Mooch couldn't see his look of contempt, and at the same time imploring him to toss a few coins their way so he and Levi could get something warm to eat. It wasn't to be, and Mooch got his first wish watching the retreating back of the man clad in heavy, warm clothing and sturdy boots.

"Bastard," he mumbled. "It's nearly Christmas. Couldn't you spare a few pounds? You could certainly afford to lose some."

He cackled at his own joke, his amusement turning to a hacking cough threatening to rip his insides out through his throat. Once his coughing fit had subsided, he hunkered down further inside his blanket and watched the few commuters passing. He was close to sleep when a soft hand fell on his shoulder, and when he looked up, the kindly face of an older woman stared at him as she pressed a five-pound note into his hand, along with a steaming cup of coffee.

"You look as if you could use this," she whispered. "I wish I could do more. You're a kid."

She smiled sadly and went on her way as Mooch managed a stuttered, "Thank you."

He grasped the cup greedily, warming his hands, and then put it down reverently as he tucked the money into his secret jeans pocket. He resisted the impulse to gulp down the coffee. He'd wake Levi up; they could share the warm drink and perhaps the five pounds might go some way towards buying them something warm to eat. Mooch scowled. He'd make damn sure it wasn't being given to Levi's supplier.

Buoyed with a sense of making the night better for them both, he leaned over and shook Levi's shoulder. Perhaps the warm coffee might put back that sparkle in Levi's green eyes and bring a faint smile to his haggard face.

"Babe? Wake up. I have coffee, and I'll go get us something to eat. It's an early Christmas present."

Levi slumbered on.

Mooch extricated his leg from under his blanket and kicked him. "Hey, sleepyhead, wake up. I need you to watch the stuff again while I get us food."

There was still no response. Mooch swore and scrambled over to pull the blanket away. He shook Levi's shoulder. "For fuck's sake, wake up."

It was only then Mooch noticed the open, bulging eyes, the open mouth clotted with vomit and the look of nothingness on Levi's face. Mooch had seen that look before.

Gut churning, he pulled off his worn woollen glove and touched Levi's face. It was ice cold, and marbled, his body as still and lifeless as a damaged mannequin tossed out into the rubbish. Mooch gave an inarticulate cry and shook Levi harder, willing him to be okay, to still be alive even though Mooch knew it was hopeless. Stricken, he noticed the needle still stuck in Levi's arm.

Mooch cried out in grief as he buried himself into the corner while pulling Levi's skinny, stiff body onto his lap. He stroked Levi's stringy, black damp hair, ignoring the puddle of cold, stodgy vomit on the blankets, currently being smeared over Mooch's clothing and hands.

"Wake up, baby," he crooned to the dead man in his arms. "I need you. Please don't leave me here. You're all I've got."

He was still sitting there clutching his friend and lover to his chest when the police arrived two hours later to take him away. One of the policemen was kind and sympathetic and told Mooch they'd take good care of him and Levi, but they needed him to come with them.

From then on Mooch knew life would never be the same again.

Chapter 1

Vomit had never been something Maxwell Lewis could stomach. However, in his job as senior flight attendant with Target Air, it was something he had to deal with ad nauseam. Faced with a rabid bull intent on eating his testicles or a whiny, crying child with pseudo-vegetable soup spewing out of his mouth, Max would take the bull anytime—even though he loved his testicles *a lot* and preferably where they were, with a man's mouth wrapped around them.

"Max, do you think you could get your head out of the clouds long enough to help me here?" The exasperated voice of fellow cabin crew colleague Fiona Randall interrupted his randy dream and Maxwell scowled.

"Fi, you know I hate this part of the job," he whined, batting his eyelashes at her. It worked sometimes, but from the look of wrath on the face of the woman in front of him, not this time.

"We *all* know how you feel about it," Fiona said, her hands busy with the bag as she tried to capture the flow of copious, foul-smelling projectile matter gushing forth from the bug-eyed kid in seat 16C. "But I think I need another bag. Do you think you can grab one?" The sarcasm in her voice made Maxwell tut as he rummaged in a nearby empty seat for an empty sick bag.

"Not helping, gurl. Sarcasm is the lowest form of wit, remember? We've had this discussion before." He pulled the bag out with a flourish and handed it over. Fiona promptly shoved the full bag of sick in his hands and he wrinkled his nose in disgust. The other passengers around him looked a little grossed out too. Maxwell popped the bag into the waste bin underneath the cart he'd been pushing down the aisle when the kid had decided to go all Vesuvius on them. He couldn't move back to the galley until Fiona had finished her clean-up operation.

A few minutes later, the kid, who turned out to be a ten-year-old unaccompanied minor, had been shuffled off to the bathroom for a wash. The area around the kid had been sanitised with air freshener and antiseptic wipes and Maxwell was pushing his near-empty trolley into the galley so he could ready it for landing.

It was a short flight and they were only fifteen minutes from touch down at Frankfurt Airport. There, Maxwell would take a twelve-hour break as he waited for the plane to fill with the next contingent of passengers and luggage. Once all were on board, he'd be flying back to London City Airport where he was based.

He loved his job mostly—the travelling, the people he met, the anonymous blowjobs in the bathroom—but he was feeling a little jaded by it all. At twenty-seven years old, he was nearing the age when both the constant travelling and the hurried sexual hook-ups were starting to lose their glitter. His favourite fuck buddy and good friend Oliver Brown was out of the running, having pledged himself to Leslie Scott, the kind of man Maxwell could only aspire to have one day.

Maxwell heaved a deep sigh, wishing he had his cute occasional-travelling-partner-in-the-air, Finchley 'Finch' Morton-Harcourt the Third, on the flight. Finch was adept at sucking Maxwell's balls down into his pink, angelic mouth and performing the blowjob of the century in the bathroom. Sometimes they used the quiet recess of the first-class cabin when it was fairly empty. Both of them had learnt to hold in their moans and gasps when they were at work. Thoughts of that greedy little mouth around his cock made him harden in his trousers and he smiled dreamily. His number one flight attendant narrowed his eyes at him.

"Max, are you ill? You have a weird expression on your face, like you have gas. Please don't tell me you're going to puke like that little horror earlier," said Grant Tooley—and yes, his boss knew all the jokes there were about his unfortunate name. Grant took a voracious glee in levelling a fierce stare at a would-be joker before ripping them to shreds with his rapier-like tongue. He also wasn't fond of children, preferring his King James spaniel, Melissa, to any human. This included his wife of three years, Annie. Maxwell never quite knew how she could play second fiddle to a yappy dog, but acceptance of her place in Grant's life was something Annie dismissed with a wry grin.

Maxwell sniffed. "I was thinking. It happens occasionally, you know. I'm not just a pretty face."

Grant snorted. "The day you think about anything more serious than whose cock you're going to suck when we land, or which guy you're going to plough next, will be the day I give up my membership in the Spaniel Appreciation Club and buy a Rottweiler." He shuddered. "Never going to happen."

Maxwell squinted his eyes at Grant in sympathy. "Are you sure you're straight? I mean, the Spaniel Appreciation Club. You sounded so gay there I thought we might be having a moment."

He evaded Grant's angry thump to his arm and hightailed it out of the gallery, narrowly missing Fiona as she carried bin bags to the disposal area.

She opened her mouth to say something, but the intercom blared and the captain's announcement they were about to descend echoed in the air. Maxwell escaped to his seat and buckled in, sticking his tongue out at his friend as he did so.

When they landed, he'd get something to eat, change his shirt, and take the time to chill out. Maybe he could even find someone to hook up with.

*****

Getting home to his studio flat around midnight was like being given a Nigella Lawson cheesecake. Maxwell loved Nigella. If he'd been straight, he might have married her, or at the very least had her as a sugar mommy. She was sexy, comforting, familiar and the very thing to make a rainy day brighter.

It was raining a May downpour as if God had smirked and flushed the celestial toilet not once but twice. Maxwell was weary and stank of sweat and puke because some old dear had heaved her insides all over his shoes soon after landing. It had obviously been National Puke on Cabin Crew Day.

He splodged into the hallway of his small, ground floor flat near the docks less than half a mile away from London City Airport, and switched on the table lamp in the narrow hallway. He left his suitcase propped against the wall. Locks of normally gelled and immaculate hair fell in wet streams down the side of his face, dribbling cold water onto his already chilled neck and back.

The area Maxwell lived in wasn't the best or safest place to live, but it wasn't too bad in his opinion. He'd been in far worse situations and could take care of himself. He'd had no trouble to date and most of his neighbours were friendly, if a little suspect.

Luckily the downpour appeared to have kept the various bad elements indoors, something for which Maxwell was thankful. Despite its uncertain location, it was still expensive, but affordable.

The flat's most attractive feature was the fact he could walk to work without relying on public transport. A friendly taxi driver called Boris occasionally gave him a lift in return for a six-pack of Sol beer. Boris hadn't been out on the route tonight so Maxwell had walked home.

And now he was pissed off. It had been a boring stopover with no envisaged hook-up because he'd fallen asleep for hours when he laid down for a quick nap. It was raining and his flat was cold—the fucking heating hadn't come on again—and the only thing cluttering his fridge was a salad that looked as if it was being terraformed.

Maxwell was fed up with coming home to an empty place.

"Yes, ladies and gentlemen, I, Maxwell Christopher Allan Lewis, past confessed slut and major player, want a man to share my life with. No one is more surprised at this revelation than I," he grumbled as he watered his half-dead pot plant. Perhaps it might rejuvenate by some kind of miracle. If not, it would be delegated to the corner of the room where so many of his other plants ended up. He could have built a compost heap with the desiccated remains of his not-so-leafy friends.

He couldn't even have a pet, for fuck's sake, because he travelled too much. He'd love a goldfish, but his friend Leslie told him fish were 'sensitive souls' and needed a lot of upkeep. Leslie's aquatic friends passed on at an alarmingly rapid rate and the man had claimed airily that 'it was just the way fish were.' Maxwell grunted. He didn't think he could cope coming home to a floating corpse in the fishbowl time and time again.

"I guess I'd have it for a *little* while at least," he muttered as he set about cleaning out his fridge and battling with the heating to turn it on. Maxwell had a bad habit of talking to himself. Sometimes, far beyond in his past, he'd been his only company and he'd broken the loneliness by holding conversations with himself. It had gotten him some trouble when he didn't pay attention to his words.

He had a weekend break now, which was a blessing. Maxwell wanted to kick back, drink, dance, fuck someone, be fucked, and try get out of the ridiculous doldrums he was in. He blamed his ex-fuck buddy Oliver and Oliver's adored boyfriend, said fish-killer Leslie, for his current mood. Seeing them so happy together had awakened something in him. The knowledge you could come home to someone special, who'd listen and be there for you when you needed them instead of being just another bonk in a bed; Maxwell wanted that emotional connection to a man so badly. It was a desire he thought had been tucked away into the murky closet of his past and not brought out in a while.

His less-than-idyllic teenage years had meant he'd learned to be self-sufficient. Having a home with heat and running water, a way to put food on the table instead of rooting in rubbish bins or begging, and a warm bed to sleep in without the demand of 'added extras' were things he would be forever thankful for despite the lack of any significant love life. Sometimes small pleasures were enough to live by.

He changed into comfortable sweats and a ragged tee shirt picked up off the sideboard in his bedroom—he didn't believe in putting all his stuff *inside* the wardrobe. He made himself a cup of coffee, and out of habit, checked his sex worksheet. Maybe he could find someone worth asking for a booty call.

This sheet, appropriately named *Sexcella* was a work of art on which he recorded most of his sexual conquests. Casual one-off relief in the plane, airports and bars for blow- or hand jobs were excluded. There were physical descriptions and pertinent details about the man in question, like the length and girth of his cock, how good his blowjob skills were, his sexual performance in actual fucking and what their potential relationship factor was. The higher Maxwell rated them overall, the odds got better he could see himself with them in a longer term relationship. He was picky; nothing less than a five suited his needs. All the men so far ranged no more than a three and a half. Finch was a three and a half. Relationship-wise, he didn't cut it. He had an understanding partner at home who didn't mind his up–in-the-air escapades as long as Finch came home to him. Maxwell didn't think he could ever be in an open relationship like that.

His list was longer than a shopping list but shorter than a listing of the Top 25 Eligible Gay
Bachelors. He'd started it years ago. He'd bigged it up to his friends and colleagues, telling them loftily it contained a lot more names than it did. It had become a self-fulfilling prophecy and he'd gone along with the game. His friends thought he was a man slut, but the reality was he'd been quite discerning in compiling it.

One day, he'd find a Five, and he'd no longer need it. Unfortunately, tonight was not the night and he couldn't even dredge up the enthusiasm to call a Four he knew.

There doesn't seem to be any point...I'm destined to be alone and horny.

Instead he switched on the television. He wasn't in the mood to play *Mass Effect* on the X-Box; he needed to alleviate some tension and watching porn was a good way to get relief. Watching Nicky Starr's porn films were even better. The man was a god. The fact Nicky was also his friend Oliver in his porn star persona didn't deter Maxwell at all. He and Oliver had had an arrangement until Leslie came along. Max didn't begrudge Oliver his new happy status; he bemoaned the lack of his own. Watching Nicky's tight, sexy body getting it on with a Leslie-like twink always made Maxwell horny. What was the fun in having a world-class adult actor as a friend and ex-fuck buddy if you couldn't watch them in action?

As Nicky pounded the twink's delectably tight and perky arse, Maxwell imagined himself sandwiched between them, seeing Oliver and Leslie in his head. He knew he was a bad boy fantasizing about his friend and his boyfriend, but he didn't care. A man had needs.

Later, sticky and sore, as he'd been rather enthusiastic in tugging his poor dick, Maxwell opened up the sleeper couch and went to bed. The jacking-off activity had done nothing to assuage the empty feeling inside him.

He drew the duvet over his head, hugged a spare pillow close to his chest and tried to forget he was sleeping alone.

Chapter 2

Gibson Henry hunkered down in his uncomfortable aeroplane seat on the aisle, scowled and made sure his earphones were tightly pressed against his ears. Even with the pounding rhythms of Black Sabbath blaring in his ears, the wails of the baby in the seat in front of him was akin to long-nailed fingers being scraped down a chalkboard. The infant's squalls sent chills down his spine, making him edgy. Depending on his mood, Gibson either listened to classical music inspired by video games, or heavy metal. Today was a heavy metal occasion.

He had to grin and bear the flight because if he ever wanted to see his family, the journey to where they lived in Cramond, outside Edinburgh, was a necessary evil. His mother, father and brother had moved up there about five years ago for his father's job. His only sibling, Richard, had insisted Gibson travel to their parents' thirtieth wedding anniversary this weekend. Their dad had been ill recently and Richard thought it would help his recovery to see his youngest son.

Gibson didn't travel well in a car, getting bored at endless hours behind the wheel without anything to keep his fingers busy. Not to mention the fact he didn't own a car anyway. Driving a hire car from Canning Town, where he lived, to the seaside village of Cramond had not been an option. Sitting on a plane he could at least work on his game design.

Gibson muttered in irritation. "I wish that kid would shut up. My damn ears are bleeding."

He ignored the look of outrage levelled by the old dowager sitting beside him and went back to his custom-designed supercharged laptop. He was working on the latest version of *Camp Queen*, a game he hoped would be another best-seller for him. Gibson was currently trying to mould the character of his sexy, wisecracking diva-assassin Phoenix Astor into something the fans would like.

There was a tap on his shoulder and he looked up in irritation. Alluring chestnut eyes framed with long lashes met his and for the first time since Gibson had boarded the plane, there was a stir of interest in his journey. The attendant looking back at him ticked all his boxes. Taller than Gibson's five-foot-four, Mr Yummy had broad shoulders and thick, coiffed rich chestnut hair swept back behind what Gibson thought were cute ears. The man sported a well-trimmed goatee framed around generous lips made for kissing or blowjobs. Gibson could *so* see them wrapped around his cock. His groin appreciated that thought too and he was glad he had his food tray down.

"Nice," he murmured.

The attendant blinked. His mouth moved and Gibson removed the earphones. "What? Sorry, didn't hear you. Mega music mix going down here."

He was flashed a wide grin. "Not a problem, sir. I asked if you wanted anything to eat." His voice was deep and well modulated. Gibson thought the guy would make a fortune on chat sex lines with the soft accent. He'd pay to listen to it.

Gibson nodded. "Are you on the menu?" Over the years, he'd been told he had no sense of decorum by friends who refused to go out with him to public places.

Luckily the guy can't clock me one here in the middle of the plane if the gaydar is off.

The attendant gave a wolfish smile. "Not today, sir. I have sandwiches or croissants though, whichever takes your fancy." One eyebrow rose in question and Gibson's jeans grew even tighter.

Fuck, this guy is cute. I'm pretty sure he's one of us too.

"Nah, I fancy something a little meatier. Something I can get my mouth around, you know?" He was pleased to see his words made the attendant swallow and close his eyes in what looked a short-lived rush of lust. The woman next to him gave a gasp of *whatever*.

Gibson grinned up at the attendant. He'd got this guy's measure. Gibson knew his slight frame, elfin face, spiky mid-length platinum hair currently streaked with red, and wire-rimmed glasses perched on his nose ticked boxes for men who liked his look. He cast his eyes down towards the man's groin and smiled. Yep, this guy was definitely one of them.

Gibson peered at the name badge on the man's lapel. "Maxwell, my man, I'm not hungry for food. I'll have an orange juice, though, if you've got one." He rummaged in his man bag and pulled out a few one-pound coins.

Maxwell nodded and selected a bottle of Tropicana from his cart. He handed it over to Gibson with a plastic cup. "Two pounds please, sir."

"That's what you guys charge for a tiny bottle like that? That's scandalous."

Maxwell shrugged his shoulders in apology and accepted Gibson's money. Their hands touched and a shock ran through Gibson.

Crap. This is such a short flight. I'm sure if was longer I'd convince him to meet me in the toilet. Maybe next time....

"Thank you. Enjoy your flight, sir. We hope to see you again soon."

"I'm sure you will," Gibson murmured. "I'll be travelling quite a bit on this airline over the next few months."

Well, he would be now he'd met Maxwell. Target had become his preferred airline of choice.

Maxwell smiled politely and moved away. Gibson made no bones about the fact he watched the attendant's arse as it made its way down the aisle. Maxwell had an exceptional derriere and Gibson could see himself between those cheeks—mouth, fingers, dick, he wasn't fussy.

Twenty minutes later the landing announcement came on, and Gibson was buckling himself up. Maxwell had walked past him a couple of times and they'd shared a few sly, knowing smiles. Gibson grinned to himself. He had a long flight coming up to attend a gaming conference in New York soon. He wondered idly if Maxwell would be on that one. He hoped so. A lot could happen on a transatlantic flight.

*****

It had been ten days since Maxwell had seen the sexy figure of Gibson Henry—yeah, he'd checked the flight manifest—aboard one of his designated flights. That platinum head was hard to miss. The red had gone but when Maxwell spotted the familiar flash of pale blond seated in 12C, his pulse quickened. The man had a preference for the aisle seats it appeared. He'd been in the galley when the passengers boarded and had missed greeting the man.

Gibson had gotten him hot and bothered from the minute Maxwell had seen him the first time. The other man's small, tight, wiry frame and pink tongue stuck out at one corner of his mouth as he focused on his laptop screen, had been all kinds of hotness. Designer glasses perched on the end of a snub nose was a particular kink for Maxwell.

And when he'd looked into those cheeky bright green eyes, Maxwell was a goner.

The 'misappropriated' Edinburgh passenger manifest had some of Gibson's personal details, which Maxwell had stored on a piece of paper in his wallet. Gibson lived in Canning Town, not far from Royal Docks; his date of birth was July 7, 1990—so he was twenty-four years old—and for good measure Maxwell now had his mobile number. He knew it was highly illegal and unethical but he'd been securing cute guys' numbers for years and no one had found him out yet. When he'd seen the man's name on the manifest for the New York flight, Maxwell had believed, like Sherlock, that the game was afoot.

Once the plane had levelled out and the drinks carts were ready to go, Maxwell made sure he was the one serving 12C. When he arrived with Ginny, his colleague, Gibson was huddled over his laptop, his face scrunched up adorably, earphones on, concentrating on some Photoshop-type programme.

Once again Maxwell tried to catch his attention by lightly tapping his shoulder. Gibson scowled, his glance upwards barely registering who was in front of him. He flapped a hand in a go-away gesture and Ginny rolled her eyes at Maxwell. They both knew passengers weren't always that polite but to see this coming from Gibson made Maxwell peeved as hell. The man hadn't even acknowledged his presence.

Huffily Maxwell moved on, smiling and joking with passengers even as he steamed with righteous anger inside. An older man in seat 21F decided he might be having a heart attack, and all thoughts of Gibson vanished in the urgency of the incident. Luckily it turned out to be gas. An hour later Maxwell finally got to see Gibson again when he delivered a drink to his fellow passenger in 12A, a stalwart man of African origins who looked as if he played rugby forward for the Teletubbies, only with muscles. Maxwell sympathised with the woman squashed between Teletubby Man and Mr Gibson 'Rude

Bitch' Henry. The woman was engrossed in her Kindle and looked up and smiled at him as he passed the drink to her seat passenger.

Gibson looked up too, and gave him an unexpected yet radiant smile. Maxwell's insides fluttered—as did something else.

The blond pulled the earphones away. "Maxwell, my man, how *are* you? I didn't know you were on this flight."

Maxwell's jaw dropped. "I was here earlier. You waved me away. Sir," he added hastily.

Gibson frowned. "I did? I was probably drawing. I tend to get grumpy when I'm doing that." He shrugged. "I don't take notice of anyone when I'm in the zone. You could literally die right before my eyes and I wouldn't give a fig."

Maxwell blinked.

Well at least Gibson Henry was honest.

"I'll try making sure I don't expire then," Maxwell said. "I'd hate to decompose while you're in the drawing *zone*."

They grinned at each other. Maxwell knew he'd better move on before he got a fierce glare from his boss for dereliction of duty.

"If I can't get anyone anything else, I'll leave you in peace." He moved away and stifled a chuckle at Gibson's *sotto voce* comment.

"What I want you can't give me right now."

Maxwell's groin heated up at the comment. He flounced his way happily down the aisle, answering passenger questions and taking drinks orders, and arrived at the galley where he began to fulfil the requests.

There was no time to make an excuse to go back to visit his cute passenger again, and finally he went on his break, having a well-deserved cup of coffee and a pastry from the cart.

When he went back to his post, it was approaching midnight. His boss for this flight, Larry Moreton, grinned at him. "Max, could you please check out Mr and Mrs Doherty in first class? Their bell went off a few minutes ago for service and I'm in the middle of sorting out another rather difficult passenger." The first-class section was surprisingly empty for a long haul flight, with a passenger quotient of eleven.

Maxwell rolled his eyes. "That old pervert and his wife? The guy goosed me earlier when I went to check on him, and his wife thought it was funny. I swear if he does it again, I'll deck him."

Larry chuckled. "You have such a cute arse. Irresistible." He pretended to inspect Maxwell's backside. "I'd fondle it." Larry was bisexual, but *so* not Maxwell's type with his smarmy pickup lines and breath smelling of pear drops. Maxwell wasn't a fan.

"Good to know. Fine, I'll see what he wants. As long as it's not me." Maxwell made his way to first class, passing Gibson on the way who winked at him.

"Hey, Max. Going somewhere?"

"To sort out a passenger in first class, sir. Can I get you anything on my way back?"

Gibson shook his head. "Nope, I have some self-service planned." He winked again. Maxwell didn't even want to begin to wonder what he meant.

He entered first class to find Mr and Mrs Doherty fast asleep. They were in their eighties, wrinkled and...old. Their service light still winked on and off and Maxwell switched it off. He crinkled his nose at the drool coming out of Mrs Doherty's thin-lipped mouth. He decided to check on the other passengers while he was there. None of them needed anything. The cabin was quiet, dimly lit and most of them were sleeping. He thought while he was there, he might as well check everything was good with the bathroom.

His hand was already on the door to open it when fingers grasped his right butt cheek and squeezed tightly.

He closed his eyes and took a deep breath as he turned around. "Mr Doherty, I'm going to have to ask—oh, it's you." A pleasant thrumming began in his cock as Gibson's hand continued to hold his arse tightly.

"I told you I was looking for self-service." Gibson's husky voice sent a shiver down Maxwell's belly to his groin. The hair on Maxwell's stomach rose with static.

Maxwell looked around. Everyone slept on and the couple of passengers who were awake were either reading, had on headphones or were watching the late-night film. No one seemed to notice the two men eye-fucking each other outside the toilet.

Gibson nodded at the door. "Open it. I'm sure we can both fit in there. I'm only a little guy—well, in height anyway." He smirked as he took his hand off Maxwell's butt and gently pulled down the lever. Raising one pale eyebrow, he motioned Maxwell inside then followed him in. It was a tight squeeze—nothing Maxwell wasn't used to, having been in this situation before—and then they were both face to face, bodies squeezed against each other. Maxwell's cock was raging to be set free and he soon got his wish.

"I doubt we have much time so we'll have to do this quickly." Gibson reached down, unzipped Maxwell's trousers and reached inside, gripping him in small, yet strong fingers. Maxwell squeaked, the feeling of a hand on his needy dick sending a jolt of electricity to his toes. He still couldn't speak.

Gibson knelt down, pushing his own loose sweats and briefs down his hips and unleashing what for his size was an impressive cock. Maxwell's mouth watered at the sight of the pink and purple cut goodness jutting up from a groin laced with blond curls. He wanted to taste it, lick it and make Gibson scream.

However, as Gibson's wet, warm mouth encircled his cock and began a slow, steady suck and pull on the head, Maxwell thought he might be the one doing the screaming. He watched the head bobbing up and down on him, and Gibson's hand curled around his own cock as he jerked himself. Maxwell tried valiantly to suppress the rising moans and groans in his throat.

He panicked after a while when he realised the door hadn't been locked and reached over to slide the lock to closed.

"Good move," Gibson said through a mouth full of cock, the reverberations of his voice tickling Maxwell's dick to new, heady heights. "And may I say, you taste as good as I knew you would. Tell me when it's time." His mouth shut up, but his eyes lifted to meet Maxwell's and the cheeky glint in those green eyes caused a head–to-toe shudder to course through Maxwell's body.

"Oh, God," he breathed, resisting the impulse to fuck Gibson's swollen, pink mouth. He didn't think it would be polite. "You're pretty good at this."

Gibson shrugged. "Practice." He leaned forward and took Maxwell deep, lips brushing his shaven pubes. Maxwell surrendered to the sensations and closed his eyes, chest heaving as he was thoroughly blown.

He'd no idea how much time had passed but the feeling of his swollen cock head brushing the back of Gibson's throat as he took him deeper was the last straw.

"Going to blow," he gasped. Gibson gave one list lick then removed his mouth. He stood up as his fingers squeezed Maxwell's dick, stroking it roughly. With a noise resembling a grunting moose in heat, Maxwell unloaded white ropes of come onto them both. Gibson gave a much manlier grunt and fisted his cock fiercely before pressing against Maxwell and unloading warm, musky fluid onto Maxwell's once pristine uniform.

They stood pressed together, gasping as bodies came down from the orgasm high. Maxwell nearly had another one on the spot as Gibson raised his fingers to his rosebud mouth and sucked off what was on them, eyes never leaving his.

"God, you are one dirty boy," Maxwell managed to get out. "You look sexy as fuck."

Gibson grinned, eyes dark and hooded. "Yes, I've been told." He pulled one finger out of his mouth with an obscene, popping sound. Maxwell couldn't even move to zip himself back up. He was boneless and on such a high, he didn't think he'd ever come down.

Gibson laughed. "Let me help you." His fingers deftly tucked Maxwell's half-hard dick back into his trousers and zipped him up. He then sorted himself out and patted Maxwell's cheek.

"Thanks. See ya."

He opened the door and was gone before Maxwell could say anything else. His jaw dropped and he stared at the empty cubicle.

What the fuck? How rude was that?

What they'd done was nothing too drastic but surely there should be some banter exchanged, perhaps even a lingering kiss— Maxwell liked kissing—before they disappeared? Maxwell had at least hoped to exchange a phone number and see if they could meet outside of being in the air. And seeing as how he was looking for something more permanent, he'd hoped…Maxwell sighed at the loss of said hope.

"I don't simply zip myself up and say 'see ya.' I have manners,'" Maxwell grumbled as he cleaned the spunk off his clothing and wiped his jacket clean with a handful of paper towel. He squinted in dissatisfaction at the papery speckled trail left behind on the fabric. His feelings were still hurt at the speed at which Gibson had left.

"I was right the first time. You *are* a rude bitch," he muttered as he left the bathroom. He took a quick glance around to see whether any of the passengers had noticed anything but they all looked much the same as when he'd gone into the bathroom—he checked his watch—ten minutes ago. It had been a record blowjob indeed. He normally took a little longer to get his rocks off.

He passed Gibson, back in his seat, earphones on, captivated once again by his laptop screen, and oblivious to Maxwell. He wondered spitefully whether he could get away with spilling a drink on the man's computer. *That* might make him sit up and take notice, especially if his balls had a chance of being fried.

Sadly, Maxwell didn't follow up on his pipedream because he valued his job. Instead, for the rest of the flight, he took to watching Gibson out of the corner of his eye, and trying not to show his in-flight sex partner he was pissed off.

Before the flight was due to land and Maxwell was on rubbish duty, he stared hard at Gibson as he packed up his laptop bag.

"Should I slip him my number or not?" he muttered. "After all, Canning Town isn't too far away from me. It's conceivable we could meet up again. Perhaps it might all work out."

Deciding on the affirmative, Maxwell wrote his number on a scrap of paper with the words 'Love to meet up again for a drink' and as he neared Gibson, he slid the folded scrap onto his lap as nonchalantly as he could. Gibson frowned, looked down at the paper, back up at Maxwell then casually pushed it back into the black bag Maxwell sported.

"Thanks but I don't do repeats," Gibson said with a shrug. "It's kind of a one-off thing, you know? Thanks anyway."

Maxwell's jaw dropped at such blatant rudeness as Gibson turned to look out of the window. Trying to hide the embarrassment of rejection, he carried on and kept the hurt off his face to show Gibson he didn't give a fuck.

Crap. He'd met his match in the flesh. *Obviously he's a tosser of note, a cocksucker, a player and in short, a douche. He is so going on Sexcella at a two rating. Great BJ. Post-coital—bleh.*

Hours later, as he tossed and turned in the bed in his hotel room on the overnight layover, the ignominy of the careless gesture still stung. He'd also decided not to participate in any more anonymous sexual escapades in the air. It was time to start thinking about his future and find someone steady he could come home to. It'd be better than a damn fish.

Chapter 3

"Fucking useless piece of shit!" Gibson threw the tablet he was using against the wall of his dining room and watched as it fell apart. It made him feel a little better.

His best friend Jack Cunningham rolled his eyes and took a sip of his beer. "You're a twat, Gib. What the fuck did you do that for?"

Gibson stormed over to the pieces on the floor and kicked them. "It's so bloody slow, and keeps freezing on me. I can't even get my mail up on it. What good is it to me?"

Jack pursed his lips and inclined his head thoughtfully. His long, brown hair swung down the sides of his face like swathes of faded velvet. "That's why I don't do tablets. Give me a laptop or a desktop any day. I mean, you can hardly even watch porn on those damn things the time they take to buffer. By the time the guy's giving it to the big tits dolly bird, it's like watching it in slow motion." He mimicked the action, making a circle of his fingers and driving another finger in and out in an exaggeratedly slow and filthy gesture. "Not worth it."

"My laptop's busy rendering some images and my desktop is downloading some new software." Gibson snapped as he paced around. "All I wanted to do was check my mail and see if Everett had got in touch." He picked up a slice of carrot from the veggie platter and bit it savagely.

"Everett the Egghead." Jack chortled. "The big, hairy, fuck buddy from Canada."

"Fuck. You." Gibson spat. "He's not that hairy. And does Beth know you make disgusting gestures like that whole finger thing you had going on?" Beth was Jack's long-time girlfriend.

Well, maybe Ev is a little hairy-like but he has a great dick and he knows what to do with it.

Everett Talbot was one of the few people Gibson fucked more than once, which was usually only once a year anyway when they attended the Gamez Geek Ultra event in Brighton. The GGU was the prestige event for game developers and designers and one Gibson never missed. Everett was also a master at coding and programming and both Gibson and Jack relied on him as one of the many freelancers they used for the development of their games.

Jack snorted. "Beth knows she's the only one for me. Doesn't mean I can't watch porn. And dude, Everett is like the epitome of a bear. Have you seen the two of you shimmying it up on the dance floor? It's like Chewbacca and Peter Pan going at it. Scary." He shivered theatrically.

Gibson narrowed his eyes. "He has a nice pelt on his chest, and a beard. What about the bird I saw you with once PB"—PB was code for Pre-Beth——"who had a damn moustache and looked as if she'd got a pair of udders on her front? No, fuck that. Double udders."

"Hey, her name was Annie, she was cool," Jack threw a disgruntled look at Gibson who stared back fiercely. "And she was a real sweetie. She had a few hormone problems at the time."

Now it was Gibson's turn to roll his eyes. "She nearly poked my eyes out when she tried to hug me. I could have died from suffocation."

The two friends glared at each other then as smiles curved their mouths, they fell into peals of laughter.

"Oh my God," Gibson managed, eyes streaming. "We had Chewy and the Pneumatic Bearded Lady as dates…"

Gibson's bad mood dissipated. Jack was always able to get him out of hissy fits by distracting him. They'd been friends forever, since secondary school. They now worked as a team in a game design company they'd formed called Anomaly Media. Jack was the writer and also a technical whizz kid at programming and code and picking out bugs. Gibson was the creative one, drawing, designing and developing the game characters and the worlds they lived in as well as coding. It was a partnership that worked well and they'd built two successful games so far, *Blockshock* and *Dust and Souls*. *Camp Queen* was Gibson's dream, his concept.

They shared the flat in Canning Town and used the spare room as their office. Jack had money behind him from a gaming business his father had owned, which saw them through the lean times—although those were not often, as their games sold well. Jack was built like a linebacker and he'd saved Gibson's arse more times than he cared to remember.

"What are you waiting on Ev for, anyway? Anything special?" Jack wiped his eyes and picked up a desiccated sandwich from the plate between them. Gibson winced as Jack munched away on dried ham and hard cheese between what looked two pieces of brown cardboard.

"Yeah. There was this b.t I couldn't get right in the animation for Phoenix and he said he thought he knew what the problem was. I sent details over to him to take a look." Gibson checked his watch. "He said he'd get back to me by three pm and it's already half past."

Jack thrust the whole half sandwich in his mouth. "Well, now you're going to have to check your damn email on my computer. Seeing as how you threw yours against the wall. Like you did with your phone the other week." His voice was non-judgmental.

Gibson sighed. He did have a tendency to get pissy when his gadgets didn't work for him. "Sorry. I'm not sure I need a tablet anyway." They smirked at each other. "I suppose I could do without for a while and use my smart phone. It's the screen is a bit small sometimes to see anything, especially all the techy stuff and I don't want to strain my eyes any more than I have to." "Whatever." Jack took a swallow of his beer, finishing it off and gave a burp as he set the empty bottle down on the table. He grinned. "Of course you could stop fucking breaking stuff, you impatient arse."

Gibson stuck a tongue out at him and Jack lunged, trying to catch it. Gibson skipped away nimbly.

"One of these days," Jack growled. "I'm gonna catch that little pink thing, rip it out and pickle it."

"Ooh, bloodthirsty," Gibson teased as he picked up the shattered pieces of his tablet. "How am I supposed to rim guys if you rip out my tongue?"

Jack's face went green. "Shit, don't put those images in my head, you bastard. I don't want to know…" his voice tailed off and he scowled and put his earphones in. A few minutes later he was swaying to what Gibson imagined was the sound of Alex Clare and the concentration on his face meant he was probably checking code.

Gibson poked him on the shoulder. "Oi. I thought you said I could check my emails?"

Jack ignored him and Gibson gave a deep sigh. It looked like he'd be relegated to using his phone to see whether Ev had sorted his problem. He wanted the issue fixed before his next flight out to Dublin to meet with an investor who was interested in promoting *Camp Queen* in his gaming boutiques and online. The demonstration needed to go well.

Thoughts of the impending flight in a week's time made him recall the brown-eyed, sexy guy called Maxwell he'd blown in the toilet on his New York flight. Gibson had to change his flight back to another airline because of a delay in NY and hadn't seen the guy again. He'd been cute and decent; Gibson had some deep-rooted guilt at blowing the guy off—no pun intended—when he'd tried to give him his number. In hindsight, it had been a shitty thing to do. The hurt in the guy's eyes had rankled a bit. Gibson might be a slut but he wasn't a cruel tosser. He'd meant to find the guy and apologise, but then he'd got sucked back into his game and that had been that.

Shoving aside his regret, he was overjoyed to find the answers he sought from Ev on his mobile, with a laconic, 'Miss you buddy, I'll be in UK in a few months and maybe we can get together' message. Gibson grinned. He'd make sure there were more Chewy and Peter Pan antics at the club to piss Jack off. Maybe a little half-naked grinding and wet bear kissing. That was sure to give his friend the heebie-jeebies.

*****

Gibson stared at his friend Cruz Castillo with growing trepidation. "Let me get this right. You want me to wear this outfit and drape myself all over your buddy Pete to make Craig prove I'm not interested in you. Is that my instruction for tonight? And how far do you want me to take it? Pete knows about this plan, yeah?" Cruz's boyfriend Craig had some crazy idea Gibson and Cruz were doing the horizontal mambo and Cruz had a plan to convince him otherwise. Pete was Cruz's friend from the gift shop where he worked as a sales assistant, and was joining them tonight at the opening of a new gay club in Soho called Innuendo.

Gibson stared at the outfit laid out on his bed and then back at his other best friend with jaundiced eyes. Cruz stared back at him, big doe eyes dark and serious, his full lips pursed.

"Sí, dipstick." It came out 'deepsteek' as Cruz's Spanish accent made itself known, normally more when he was stressed. "Pete will play along. If Craig sees you with Pete dressed like *that*"—he waved a slim, brown hand and bit his lip imploringly—"he will *have* to believe I am not interested in you or you in me 'that way.'"

Gibson huffed and glanced down at the outfit with a sense of unease. The silver hot pants complemented his hair, although they would cover virtually nothing of his arse or his hips. And as for his dick…he shivered. He was cut, and wearing those, the whole world would know about it. The black mesh tee shirt with straps and buckles was, well, tight, but wearable. As were the shoes. A pair of glittery, two-inch-high silver boots, with red laces, which he thought he was supposed to tie around his calves.

Cruz sighed. "It's a theme evening tonight, bebé. Gladiators and Glad Rags. You don't own anything like this so I had to borrow this outfit from someone for you. I couldn't loan you any of my clothes or Craig would think we are together."

"Tell me again how making Craig think I'm fucking someone else when I'm not is going to help you get him back?" Gibson and Cruz had never had that sort of relationship; Cruz was like his brother, but for some reason, Cruz' ex had never accepted it. The pair had had a heated argument over it a week ago.

Cruz rolled his eyes and blew a strand of ink-black hair off his forehead. "Because he will see you and Pete making out, and I will be like"—he draped a dramatic hand to his forehead—"I don't care, I want you, and Craig will realise what he is missing and that he adores me, and then we will make mad, passionate love at the club."

Gibson thought there might be a flaw in this plan somewhere. "And Pete isn't going to take this too far, is he? I mean, you said he's a nice guy but I don't want to have to get serious with him."

"Sexy dancing, bumping, your usual slutty stuff," Cruz said helpfully.

Gibson scowled. "Yeah, thanks for that." He heaved a sigh. "Fine, I'll do it. You are *so* going to owe me one."

Cruz's face sparkled with a smile showing off white teeth. "Thank you, sweetie. I love you." He leaned forward and planted a smacking kiss on Gibson's cheek. "Now I need to go home and get ready. I'll meet you outside Innuendo at nine. I have our VIP tickets so we don't need to queue, but I left them at home." He waved goodbye and flounced out of the bedroom.

Gibson heard him calling to Jack. "Bye, Het Man, please make sure Gibson gets dressed on time."

Gibson suppressed a grin at Jack's snarl at his hated nickname. Cruz loved to tease him. Jack loved superheroes and had often enquired plaintively why he couldn't be 'Muscle Man' or 'Sex God' rather than 'Het Man.'

Hours later, after showering, man-scaping, shaving and moisturising, making sure he could fit all his man bits into the clothes he was wearing, Gibson was ready. He looked in the mirror and took a deep breath.

The man looking back at him was willowy, yet toned, with broad shoulders and strong muscled arms from swimming.

Gibson might be short but he was all in proportion. His fair-skinned legs were devoid of hair—he only had faint blond wisps on them even when he didn't shave—and his mousse-styled platinum hair was artfully sculptured. He'd changed his glasses to his clubbing pair, a trendy pair of dark silver frames, which enhanced his green eyes. He couldn't wear contacts; his eyes were too sensitive to use them for long.

He twisted around and gave a grin when he observed his arse in the mirror. Tight and perky. Just the way he liked it—and others did too. There was quite a lot of his cheeks and crack on show but there was nothing he could do about it. He sat on the bed, and pulled on the boots, wrapping the long laces around the bottom of his legs.

For good measure, he slid in a barbell to his pierced belly button. The shirt and shorts didn't meet over his stomach, leaving a vast expanse of pale, toned skin and the start of a four pack, of which he was quite proud. He popped another earring into his ear and wrapped a few leather bracelets around his wrist. The final look was damn sexy, slutty and, even if he said it himself, mighty fine. He pursed his lips in the mirror and blew himself a kiss.

"Pete, my man, you are not going to know what hit you tonight. Make sure you know the boundaries or I'll have to kick you in the nuts."

He picked up his bum bag, stuffed in what he needed and hot-footed it into the hallway. He ran into a muscled man mountain on his way out and gave a startled cry.

"Jack, I didn't know you were still here. I thought you'd gone to Beth's." Beth was Gibson's favourite lady other than his mother. He liked the spritely red head.

Jack stepped back, his eyes wide, mouth open in what looked like gob-stopping alarm.

"Gib, what the hell? You can't go anywhere dressed like that. Someone will kick your arse." He pushed long hair behind his ear as he stared at his friend in trepidation.

"Who are you, my mother?" Gibson said in irritation. "What the hell?" He pushed his glasses up his nose with his middle finger, hoping Jack got the hint.

Jack's eyes roved down his body in disbelief. "You…you have hardly anything on. I mean, I can see your damn dick, like..." His Adam's apple bobbed as looked at Gibson in dismay.

Gibson threw him a fierce stare. "Yeah, what about it? It's a Gladiator party, and I, my man, am one sexy gladiator." He twirled around and took great glee seeing Jack looking ready to faint. "Come on, you've seen me in club wear before. What's the big deal?"

"Not like that." Jack's voice was faint. "I mean—half your arse is hanging out."

"All the better to feel me up, or stick it in," Gibson quipped.

Jack blanched and Gibson took pity on him.

"Oh for God's sake. I'm wearing my long coat over this outfit. You didn't think I'd get on the tube dressed like this, did you? Credit me with a little bit of sense."

He stomped into the entrance and grabbed his long trench coat off the peg.

Jack's eyes narrowed. "Well, 'scuse me for worrying my best friend is going to be fresh twink bait for the bears and haters out there. The coat makes you look like a damn flasher."

"Jack, I'll be fine, promise. I'll get a lift home anyway, if I come home. I might get lucky and it's Saturday tomorrow, so no work. I'll text you, though, if I don't come home." He shrugged into his coat and fastened it.

"You'll have them lining up to do you that the way you look tonight," Jack grumbled.

Gibson narrowed his eyes. "You know, I might think you were jealous if I didn't know you were a very straight man and my best buddy since forever. What gives?"

He was shocked to see Jack looked apprehensive. They usually teased each other about Gibson's lifestyle but not to this extent.

"Have you been watching the news lately?" Jack asked quietly, all traces of teasing gone from his tone. "Every time you switch it on lately there's something about some gay or lesbian being bullied or beaten."

Gibson sighed. "Sure, it happens. I can't live my life worrying about it though."

"I worry about you. I'm a big guy; people think twice about trying to take me down. But a little shit like you…"

Gibson's heart ached and he stepped forward and laid a hand on Jack's arm. "Hey, nothing is going to happen to me." He motioned to his bag. "I have a whistle, a can of Mace Cruz gave me, and I can run fast. I'm prepared."

Jack's eyes were still shadowed. "Please be careful, Gib. That mouth of yours can sometimes run away with you too and I'd hate for you to attract some wanker's attention." He grimaced. "Especially given what you're not wearing. Promise me you'll watch out for yourself."

"I will," Gibson promised. A surge of affection at his friend's concern made him lean forward and kiss Jack's cheek. "I have no desire to become a victim. "He punched Jack on the arm. "'Sides, I'll sic you on him afterwards if anyone tried anything. And no one wants the Sex God coming down on his sorry arse."

Jack looked unconvinced. "Let me know if you stay out or I'll worry."

Gibson nodded and crossed his chest. "Scout's Honour."

"You were never a scout, half pint," Jack said with a slight smile.

Gibson pouted. "Neither were you, Het Man." He dodged Jack's punch and flung open the door. "I'll text you if I get lucky," he yelled as he made his way to the lifts.

He didn't have time to hear what Jack shouted after him as he stepped into the lift and the doors closed.

Chapter 4

Maxwell stood sipping his strawberry daiquiri as he watched the dancers writhing on the dance floor. The new club was heaving and he already regretted coming. He'd been given a ticket by a friend, and if he hadn't used it said friend would be as pissed as hell. The tickets were rare, like a Willy Wonka chocolate bar.

Maxwell was quite a fan of dress-up, but he thought the Gladiators and Glad Rags event sounded a little ambitious for a collection of ragtag patrons dressed in cut-off sheets and leather belts and straps across sweating bodies. He'd tried his best though. He looked down at his own outfit. He'd spent some of his hard-earned pennies online to get himself a passable tunic crested with gold thread and a pair of Roman sandals. A sword and dagger had been offered with it but he'd not had the money to waste for those. His hair was styled into some semblance of mussed-up magnificence and he'd trimmed his goatee to a light shadow. His hairy, muscled legs stuck out from his short tunic and had already gotten a lot of lip-licking attention. He'd had a few offers tonight. First, he'd been hit on by a huge guy he'd nicknamed Bearzilla; dressed in full Roman regalia, he'd been looking for a willing sub for the night. While Maxwell wasn't averse to the idea usually, Bearzilla wasn't his idea of someone he wanted holding him captive.

The guy who'd approached Maxwell afterwards hadn't been great either, as he'd been with his partner, looking for a third. He'd been spaced out and Maxwell knew the guy was on something. The one thing Maxwell had no tolerance for were drugs and people on drugs. He had a pathological hatred of them and anyone who dealt them. He didn't even like taking medicine.

Maxwell's recent dissatisfaction with the way his love life, or lack of it, was turning out made him wonder if anyone else here tonight was looking for the same thing: a little stability in a relationship and not a series of one-night stands.

He muttered to himself, "Hell, yeah right. Like that's going to happen. I shouldn't have even come here tonight. I should find a Scrabble club somewhere, maybe a ball-dancing group. That's more likely to deliver dividends for the start of a relationship than this place."

He stared idly out at the crowd, noticing a small, sexy, blond-haired guy in silver micro shorts grinding against a tall, well-built Asian man. The blond was familiar in some way, cock-stirringly tasty and very much Maxwell's type; he even wore glasses. The Asian guy was hands on and Maxwell grunted. It was what you'd expect in a club like this, but he wished it was his hands all over the blond's pert little arse. He mused whether to go over and cut in, thinking he might as well have fun while he was here and who knew? Perhaps the guy was looking for something a little longer term.

He was about to make a move when he saw the Asian guy's hand reach down and grip the blond man's crotch. Maxwell sniggered when the smaller man pulled away, stomped on the other man's foot with his silver boots, not once, but twice. He snapped something, pushed the grimacing man away then whirled to make his way towards the bar. As he drew nearer, Maxwell's heart stopped.

"Gibson?" God, the man was sex personified up close. Maxwell's cock swelled under the tunic, his mouth watering at the vision of a pale-skinned, pale-haired pixie with a scowl on his face and green eyes flashing anger at the world.

Gibson didn't appear to hear him and gestured to the bartender. "Dan, can I have a Vampira please?" He took off his glasses and started cleaning them with a bar napkin.

The bartender nodded. "Sure, honey. One Vampira coming up."

Gibson put back his glasses, tapped his fingers impatiently on the bar and the slow burn of something dark welled in Maxwell's chest.

Doesn't he even recognise me? Am I that unmemorable?

"You don't remember me, do you?" He stood a little closer.

Gibson frowned and peered through glasses already steaming up again. "You do look familiar—wait—oh, Maxwell, right? From the plane? Wow, small world. How are you?" He shrugged apologetically. "Sorry, my glasses were mucky earlier from dancing. I couldn't see properly."

Maxwell was gratified Gibson at least remembered his name. "Yeah, that's me." He gestured towards the floor. "Looked like you handled yourself okay out there with that guy."

Gibson rolled his eyes. "Yes, he's okay but he was getting a bit too hands on. I warned him not to take the bloody charade too far but did he listen? Nooo…"

He smiled at Dan, took the drink the bartender gave him and slid a ten-pound note across the counter.

"Charade?" Maxwell watched as Gibson slid the change into the white leather bag he had strapped around his hips. A belly bar twinkled in the light and Maxwell was mesmerised by the sexy shimmer. And the flat, toned stomach it belonged to. And the cheeky curve of Gibson's arse.

"Yeah. I'm here, dressed like this, which isn't my usual outfit by the way, dancing with Pete, to make *that* guy realise I'm not having it on with my gbf." Gibson gestured towards a couple on the dance floor, a short, dark-skinned guy in his early twenties who was busy excavating the contents of the mouth of a broad-shouldered black guy dressed in leather.

"Gbf?" Maxwell said in bemusement.

"Gay best friend." Gibson sucked at his drink through the straw and Maxwell was mesmerised by the sight of pink lips around a candy cane piece of plastic. "He's the little guy. Craig is his ex-boyfriend, but from the looks of it, whatever I was doing with Pete worked. They look as if they're enjoying themselves and hopefully Craig now realises I'm not into Cruz."

They watched in companionable silence as the two dancing men's groins undulated against each other, and as their kissing on the dance floor grew even hotter.

"Christ, I shouldn't be watching them," Gibson grumbled. "It's making me hard and in these shorts that's a bad idea. My dick might split the seams these things are so tight."

At those careless words, Maxwell's cock flagged to attention harder and more aching than before. A quick flick down towards Gibson's groin confirmed he clearly didn't have much room to manoeuvre.

"You got some time off from flying then?" Gibson cocked his head with a knowing grin, probably having seen the direction of Maxwell's eyes.

"I have a whole three days off before my next shift. I heard about this place opening, decided to check it out. It's pretty cool."

"Yeah, lots of new talent." Gibson gave a noisy slurp of his drink then peered at Maxwell over his glasses. Maxwell's stomach clenched in appreciation.

"I don't normally do this, but do you fancy a repeat? There's a bathroom on the left we can slip into."

Maxwell drew in a deep breath. He was *so* going to regret this, he knew it. He had to take a stand somewhere though in his search for everlasting love.

"Thanks, but no. You're not the kind of guy to get involved, or so you said when you blew me off last time, so it wouldn't solve any purpose except for a quick bit of pleasure. I wasn't really in the mood for this tonight but I promised a friend." He drank up what was left of his cocktail and put the empty glass on the bar.

Gibson looked shame faced. "Yeah, about that. I'm sorry. I shouldn't have been such a git. I wanted to apologise to you on the plane afterwards but then things ran away with me and I got distracted."

Maxwell was heartened by the apology. That took balls. "No problem. I understand. I'm at a bit of different path in my life. I'm tired of the fuck 'em and suck 'em. I want someone to come home to. Maybe it's a stupid pipe dream but I have to start trying to find someone somewhere, right?"

He smiled at Gibson, who stared back at him with a strange expression.

I bet he isn't used to being turned down. Maybe I'm being an idiot.

Maxwell wondered if his newfound principles were worth it. He might have to reconsider.

Someone shoved against Gibson, causing his drink to go flying all over the back of another man standing at the bar— a very big man in a shiny dress suit, flashy jewellery and what looked like a permanent scowl etched on his wide face. He turned around and grabbed Gibson's wrist, causing him to cry out softly in pain.

"What the fuck? You've messed up my suit," Shiny Suit growled.

Gibson tried to wrench his wrist free. "Hey, you ape, let go of me. I'm sorry, it was an accident. Someone knocked me."

"Yeah? Fucking twinks. You think all you have to do is bat your girly eyelashes and a man will forgive you anything. I ought to—"

"Let him the fuck go," Maxwell said evenly. His blood was heating up like lava in Pompeii at seeing Gibson being manhandled. His temper was slow to burn but when it did, oh boy. Maxwell was quick to go from slow denotation to supernova I'm-going-to-fuck-you-up-so-badly status. He controlled it—mostly. When he'd been on the streets, it had taken all his self-control not to become an animal like some of his friends had. And sometimes an animal had been what you needed to be to get by.

"What did you say to me?" Shiny Suit's lips twisted. "Punk, you think you can take me on?" He let go of Gibson, who stood rubbing his wrist with a worried expression.

"Max, leave him. He's not worth it. He's a douche bag in a suit. Let's get out of here—" Gibson's voice was cut off as the other man reached out and slapped him on the cheek, the flat sound echoing in Maxwell's ears like the knell of doom. Behind the bar, Dan motioned to the bouncers across the room to come over.

The rushing blood in Maxwell's ears grew to rock-concert crescendo and he moved forward in front of Shiny Suit, standing between him and Gibson. At the sight of a red handprint on Gibson's fair skin, and the look of shock on his face, Maxwell now wanted to hit someone. He took a deep, centred breath to calm himself down. The last thing he wanted to do was scare Gibson away.

"I might look all soft and cuddly," Maxwell murmured, "but beneath this gorgeous and drool-worthy exterior lies the heart and soul of a primal beast."

Shiny Suit's eyes widened in confusion and Maxwell thanked the gods he seemed to have a dumb one here. Brawn and no brains were always so much easier to bring down. Years of fighting his own battles against bullies at school, hanging out with street gangs and learning to fight dirty had often proven his salvation at times like these.

And there was one way he'd found to distract a bully and calm himself down that was almost fool proof.

He adopted his *Karate Kid* stance—the Crane Kick. He stepped back, curling his arms and hands into position. Gibson's face was a picture in astonishment and Shiny Suit looked confused. Maxwell lifted his one leg and gave a blood-curdling screech. The bully stepped back with a look of panic.

Out of the corner of his eye, Dan the bartender was laughing like a loon. Maxwell had no idea where the bouncers were but hoped they'd get here soon before he had to kick arse. Immediately around him, the crowd had hushed and faces stared at him in anticipation.

"What the hell, are you fucking crazy?" Shiny Suit looked around the bar as if asking for someone else to agree with him.

Maxwell did. "Why yes indeed, kind of you to notice. I'm the baddest motherfucker you ever laid eyes on and if you don't apologise to my friend for hitting him, right now, I'm going to kick the ever-mighty shit out of you."

Gibson's eyes were like green dinner plates. "Maxwell, are you sure you're okay? Did you take something?"

"No I bloody didn't," Maxwell huffed, straining to keep his position. His upraised leg ached and he was sure his signed Andrew Christians were showing under the tunic. "I want this arsehole to say he's sorry for being such a dickhead. Quickly. Before my foot finds his knackers and pushes them into his throat."

Shiny Suit looked down at his groin and winced.

The man next to him, a slim, older man, clutched his arm. "Chris, apologise and forget it. The guy didn't do it on purpose and I can clean your suit, baby." He tugged at Chris's arm and Chris scowled.

"Running out of patience, people," Maxwell growled. In reality, his leg was aching. "Either say sorry to my buddy here or face the wrath who is Maxwell Unleashed."

Gibson's mouth framed the words, 'Maxwell Unleashed.'

The sight of his name on those beautiful lips and the adorable look of stupefaction on Gibson's face made Maxwell determined to follow through his threat. He gave another yowl and kicked out his foot, narrowly missing Chris's groin. "Next time I connect," he yelled.

Chris was yanked back by his seemingly irate partner. "For God's sake, let's go. I want a drink and a dance, say the fuck you're sorry already, you buffoon."

Chris stared at Maxwell then at Gibson then at the bouncers who now stood beside him, arms folded, waiting to see what happened next. Chris seemed to know when he was beaten.

"Fine," he spat, turning to Gibson. "I'm sorry I hit you. Take your crazy friend away from me, and let's call it a night, right?"

He turned and was pushed through the crowd by his partner who mouthed a 'Sorry, guys' as he left.

Maxwell put his leg down and watched them go with a smirk. Around him, people started clapping and cheering, and he grinned and took a bow. He stood up quickly as he realised doing that showed his arse to the world. "Thanks, my esteemed audience. Glad I could entertain you."

"Hey, crazy guy. These are on the house." Two huge cocktails stood on the bar. Dan was chuckling fit to bust a gut. "Your boyfriend is one lucky guy. That was some crazy shit you pulled there for him."

"He's not my boyfriend," Maxwell said, a little longingly. "He's a—" He didn't even have time to decide whether he was going to say friend or fuck buddy when he found his lips being claimed by a soft, searching pair. Gibson framed Maxwell's face in long fingers and kissed the crap out of him. Maxwell yielded—he was only human after all—and all sound ceased until there was only the scent and feel of the man pressed against him. His glasses dug into Maxwell's cheek but he didn't give a fig.

He tried not to get too handsy; Gibson did have boots on, after all, and wasn't scared to use them. But the feel of the smaller man in his arms, his lean torso and kissable lips and the hardness pressed against his groin led to a memorable moment indeed.

When he was released and Gibson stepped back, lips swollen and wet, Maxwell tried to gather his brains back into his head from his crotch so he could form a sentence. He was still trying to when Gibson spoke.

"What you did for me back there…no one's ever done something like that for me before. Well, apart from Jack. He's my sbf."

"Sbf?" Maxwell was proud he'd managed to speak three whole letters. And what was it with this guy and all the acronyms?

"My straight best friend. You are one insane dude. That guy could have hurt you."

Maxwell shrugged. "When you've lived on the streets, you learn how to take care of yourself."

Gibson drew a shocked breath. "You were on the streets?"
Crap. I didn't mean to let that out. Best gloss over it.
"Yeah. So, you kissed me."

Gibson smiled slowly. Maxwell's heart gave a ping and beat faster.

Gibson grinned. "Yes. Problem?"

"Hell no. Best kiss I've ever had."

Gibson looked shy. "Thanks. I like kissing."

"It's one of my favourite things to do too." Maxwell leaned over and gently kissed Gibson's cheek where the pale pink of the slap still showed.

Gibson drew in a soft breath and Maxwell was sure as they looked at each other in the clamour of the club, and only having eyes for each other, that they'd had 'a moment.' From the uncertain look on Gibson's face, Maxwell wondered if he was mistaken.

He'd be upgrading Gibson to a resounding four and three quarters on his spreadsheet, based on his kissing skills alone. The small deduction was because he needed to leave some room for improvement and maybe, with time, he might get there. If Gibson was into a repeat performance and wasn't going to break his heart. Because Maxwell knew now, after *that* kiss, if Gibson asked for a visit to the loo, despite what Maxwell's brain said, his heart and little head would say 'Hell yeah.'

He picked up the cocktail, passed one to Gibson then picked up his own and took a sip. "Here's to crazy men doing crazy things in nightclubs."

"I'll drink to that." Gibson smiled and they toasted each other. The pang in Maxwell's chest morphed into something larger, an ache making him want to bottle Gibson in a fairy jar and never let him go. The man, with his pale green eyes, freckled nose and wavy blond curls, had crept into his heart. For a while they stood at the bar observing the activity around them.

Gibson shot him a shy smile. "I know it's late but I've got nowhere to be in the morning. You said no already but that was before you went all Mr Miyagi. Do you want to go somewhere quieter with me, we could talk, get to know each other a bit more?" He fidgeted as Maxwell gazed at him.

Maxwell's brain was adamant. *He's going to break your heart. You should say no. Say no. Just like that. It's easy.*

He nodded without even realising it. His heart and little head were all too convincing.

I don't care anymore about finding 'the one.' I want him. *Even if it's only for tonight.*

"Sure. We can go to my place if you like. It's not too far." Maxwell's inner common sense hung its head in shame and despair.

Gibson beamed brightly as he took out his mobile from his waist bag. "I need to let my friends know I'm leaving. They'll be rabid they missed all the fun." He finished his drink. "They're probably in the bathroom. I think I saw them disappear before this all kicked off." He hesitated. "While I have my phone out, do you want to give me your number again? I promise I'll keep it."

Maxwell recited his number and watched Gibson key it in, all the time studying how his face scrunched up in concentration. The guy was adorable, sweet under that glossy exterior and not as confident as he looked. And he was all Maxwell's for one night.

He could live with that.

He could always start his search for true love again tomorrow.

Chapter 5

Gibson was both thankful and nervous when they got back to Maxwell's home at close to midnight. The taxi ride home had been a quiet one, neither man sharing much or talking. Once or twice Maxwell had smiled at him then turned to look absently out of the window. He looked to be regretting his decision and Gibson wasn't sure if he should call it a night. But he'd already texted Jack to let him know there was a possibility he'd only be home in the morning so he may as well see how the night played out.

Maxwell's flat was in a fairly dodgy part of the city, but it was small, cosy and looked as if a crazy Tasmanian devil had whirled through it and dislodged everything either onto the floor, or onto the top of any available surface. Gibson hung up his coat then stared around at the room, trying not to cringe over the discarded clothing, empty pizza boxes, half-filled cool-drink glasses, book stacks, piles of clothing stacked high and remnants of what looked like a nursery of dead plants and pots in the corner of the room.

Maxwell saw him looking and he chuckled. "Yeah, I'm a bit of a slob. Sorry. I don't get much time off, and I'm flying around so much I tend to leave the housekeeping for when I'm in the mood. Which is never."

"What's with the dead foliage?" Gibson waved towards the poor dried-out sticks. "It looks like a graveyard."

Maxwell laughed. "I have a tendency to kill anything green. I've been toying with the idea of getting a fish to keep me company but I'm scared it'll die too."

He walked over to the open plan area serving as a kitchen with a small cooker, hotplate and under-counter fridge. Utensils littered the countertops, and in the corner there was a random, mismatched set of crockery. On top of the cooker sat a frying pan and one small saucepan. It looked as if most of what Maxwell owned was actually out on display. Gibson hoped he wasn't some crazy hoarder person who might keep him locked up somewhere. His nerve endings tingled at that thought.

Maxwell turned to him. "Do you want anything to drink? I think I have a bottle of wine somewhere in here."

Gibson nodded. "If you have some, I'll have a glass. Thanks."

He sat down gingerly on the two-seater couch, after moving half a dozen tatty books and a box set of *Dexter* DVDs, something which made his skin prickle even more, into a neat pile on the floor. Gibson carefully laid out the pieces of Maxwell's airline uniform, currently draped across the back of the couch he wasn't sitting at.

Maxwell came over and handed him his drink. "Sorry, I don't have wine glasses, so the tumbler will have to do."

He sat down next to Gibson, leaning back against the clothing, and placed his own drink onto the side table, which was no mean feat as it was filled with *Men's Health* magazines and a snow globe of London Bridge.

For a minute there was an uncomfortable silence.

"You like your stuff around you, I see." Gibson waved a hand around the room. "It makes sense having it all to hand. You never have to wonder where you put it." He'd meant it as a joke. His own place was pristine, orderly with everything in its place, and to him this screamed chaos—but he appreciated others might not be the same.

Maxwell's face shadowed. "Sorry. I know it looks messy, but I'm not good at being tidy. You're right. I do like to see my stuff around rather than packed away."

"That wasn't a criticism, Maxwell. Only an observation." He stretched lazily, rejoicing when he saw Maxwell's eyes darken. Maxwell's heated gaze dropped to Gibson's legs, eye fucking them downwards then back upwards to Gibson's groin. The hunger on his face turned Gibson's insides to soft mush and his dick began rising in his tight shorts. A slight smile formed on Maxwell's face.

"God, you are so sexy," he murmured as he reached out and brushed the back of his hand down Gibson's smooth thigh. "The first time I saw you I knew you were going to be a handful."

"More than a handful, I hope," Gibson whispered as he set his drink down, took off his glasses and watched through blurry eyes as Maxwell's hand trailed up and down his skin. He burned with that sensual touch and wanted to get out of his shorts post haste. He had visions of his dick ripping through the fabric like one of the monsters in *Alien*.

When Maxwell's hand brushed his groin, he hissed, his breath quickening, and he couldn't help the involuntary push of his hips towards Maxwell's hand. That hand reached down and unzipped him as sienna-brown eyes focused on his. Maxwell drew a hitchy breath, realising Gibson wore nothing underneath the shorts. His tongue came out to lick his lips and Gibson lost his breath at the erotic sight.

"I couldn't wear anything under these," he whispered, throat dry. "Hey me, easy access."

Maxwell's fingers stroked his cock, rubbing his thumb over the head, and Gibson let out a soft exhale of breath as he closed his eyes and focused on the slow strokes across his sensitive skin. When something hot and wet licked at him, he moaned and opened his eyes to see Maxwell's tongue swiping slow licks up and down his cock.

"Oh…" he was breathless with the teasing assault of his most sensitive bits.

Maxwell chuckled huskily. "You taste good…I love that you shaved here." He took Gibson in, tongue slicking up and down, his mouth hollowing as he sucked Gibson's brains out. Gibson didn't want to push or be rude, but he so badly wanted to fuck Maxwell's mouth until he came.

He was no stranger to blowjobs, but the way Maxwell treated him, as if he were something precious, sent thrills down his spine and a tingling hum across his skin. Gentle fingers cradled his balls as Maxwell pleasured him, rubbing his taint, and Gibson slid further down on the couch, opening his legs and allowing his partner access to that most hidden of places. He wanted to feel a finger or two in his arse and his current position prevented it. He tugged at Maxwell's hair, urging him upwards, and the man currently feasting on him looked up. His pupils were blown, his mouth wet with pre-come and saliva. Gibson nearly came from the debauched sight.

"I need to get these off," Gibson gasped, as he stood up and pushed his shorts down his legs. For good measure he removed the rest of his clothing and stood naked before Maxwell.

"That's better," Gibson purred and pulled Maxwell to his feet. His lips found Maxwell's and he thrust his tongue inside his mouth, tasting himself on Maxwell's lips. Hands gripped his arse, and Gibson wrapped his legs around the man holding him.

"You need to get naked too," Gibson murmured as his teeth grazed Maxwell's shoulder and bit down softly. "I'm not fucking a man in a dress."

The low laugh in his ear made Gibson's groin ache.

"I'm going to have trouble doing that while you're wrapped around me like a damn octopus." Maxwell set Gibson down on the floor. "Let me get this off then. And there'll be no fucking tonight."

Gibson gasped in horror. "No fucking?" His lips formed a pout. "Don't you want me?" He'd never been refused a fuck before.

Maxwell shrugged off the tunic and slid his briefs down his legs to land on the floor. "I think *this* proves I want you." '*This*' was an impressive erection: an uncut, beautiful, upright cock Gibson drooled over. "Let's take things easy first."

He sat back on the couch and motioned to Gibson. "Get over here. On my lap."

Gibson was still a little miffed but he wasn't going to argue. He straddled Maxwell, pressing and grinding against him. Maxwell's groan of pleasure and the fact his cock was velvet-wrapped steel as they frotted like teenagers made Gibson's hole ache to be filled.

He knelt up, leveraging himself down so they were still joined but Maxwell had access to his arse. "Put your fingers in me, Max." Maxwell's pupils blackened at Gibson's use of the diminutive.

Note to self. Maxwell likes that name.

Gibson moved Max's hand to his arse. "Please, Max. I want to feel you inside me while we do this."

Max moaned. "I need lube, Gibson. I'm not doing you dry. I have some somewhere…" His hand groped around the sofa and finally he found what he was looking for.

Gibson chuckled. "There's a definite bonus to you having your stuff all over the place." He watched as Max opened the tube and squirted its contents into his hand. "Now do me. I want to see you get off like this while you have your fingers inside me."

Max stared at him, eyes unfocused. "God, the things you say…"

They kept up the momentum of rubbing against each other as Max slid cold lube against the crease of Gibson's hole. Staring into each other's eyes, Gibson cried out softly as a finger pushed into him. Every forward stroke he took in their sensual play made his senses swim and every downward movement pushed Max's finger deeper inside him. One finger became two, two became three and soon Gibson was riding those fingers like a man possessed while his cock threatened to burst.

"Oh, fuck." His movements became frenzied as Max thrust upwards harder, biting his lip as their cocks rubbed together. His fingers sparked something inside Gibson, making him cry out in pleasure. A tingle in his backside and groin heralded his orgasm.

"God, you are gorgeous," Max whispered as he found Gibson's lips and a greedy tongue filled his mouth.

With a sputtered cry and a surrendering of his body to the tremors giving him release, Gibson came all over Max's stomach and chest, fronds of come hitting his lover's jaw and lips. Max gave a deep groan and warmth flooded Gibson's nether regions in a sticky and musky-scented explosion.

Gibson collapsed against Max, aware there were still fingers up his arse. He liked the sensation of being claimed and owned by this man. This man who'd stood up for him a crowded club against another man who could have pulverised him. It was something he didn't want to analyse too much right now, as it was a little scary. He wasn't used to feeling this way.

He winced as the fingers slid out of him and Max caressed Gibson's flank with hands still sticky from lube and Gibson's own fluids. The soft stroking soothed Gibson and he closed his eyes as he lay sandwiched against Max's sticky and faintly hairy chest.

"That was epic," Max sighed. He shifted and leaned down to kiss Gibson's belly, lips lingering on his belly bar. "This is so damn sexy. So damn you."

Gibson nodded drowsily then shivered. "I'm cold…is there something wrong with your heating?"

Max scowled. "It's probably gone off again. I can't get the hang of the bloody thermostat. Budge off me, baby, let me get you warmed up."

Gibson raised an eyebrow at the 'baby' but let it go. Reluctantly he rolled onto the couch and watched Max push himself up and walk over to the control on the wall. The man had a very nice arse himself, round and tight, and…

"Oh my God, you have a tattoo!" The sight of the scorpion on Max's right hip, about three inches in length and one wide, was unexpected. Sexy, but not something he'd expect from this man who was mostly snark and witty repartee. He'd expected butterflies or God forbid, a *Kung Fu Panda*.

Max didn't reply as he fiddled with the thermostat and then walked back to the couch, half-hard dick swinging before him and showing a nice set of balls. He stopped in front of Gibson.

"Yeah," Max said, his face guarded. "A remnant from my teenage years."

Gibson stood up and traced the tattoo. "It looks like a gang tattoo," he mused. "Like one of those you'd see in some bad-arse street gang. Is that writing on there?" He leaned down and peered at it. A faint line of text mirrored the line of the scorpion's upraised tail. "*Acculeum in cauda*," he said aloud.

He stared at Maxwell. "What does it mean?"

Max opened a drawer to the side table and picked out a pack of wet wipes. He pulled the tag back, took out a handful and began wiping himself down. He handed the pack to Gibson. His eyes were distant and Gibson wondered what he'd said to cause the change in mood.

"It's Latin. It means 'the sting in the tail.'"

"The sting in the tail," Gibson repeated. He frowned. "What does it mean?"

Max shrugged. "Scorpions sting with their tails. That's about it. Nothing deeper."

"You don't have to tell me." Gibson said quietly as he wiped off the spunk from his belly. "I don't want to pry. You hardly know me well enough to share stuff." The pang in his chest as he said that made him realise how true that was.

Something is off here. I actually want to know him better. That's never happened before.

Max's eyes narrowed. "It's not that." He looked at Gibson's arms, which were goose bumped. "You're cold and it's late. Do you want to get into bed? It's warmer there."

Gibson was seeing another side to the man before him. Gone was the sexy, affable buffoon, and in its place was a wary-eyed, cautious stranger. But he was cold and bed sounded good. He didn't want to make his way home this early in the morning. And the thought of sleeping next to Max was strangely appealing. Gibson didn't do that with his pick-ups.

"I guess. Where's the bedroom?"

"You're looking at it." Max remarked drily, with a hint of the man he'd been before. "This is a poor man's flat. I'm a lowly flight attendant after all, not a dot-com geek."

Gibson frowned. "I'm a character artist, not a dot-com geek. I design computer games, do the animation and such."

Max's ears seemed to prick up as he pushed everything off the couch onto a pile on the floor and set about opening the bed out. Gibson wanted to huff in protest after all the trouble he'd taken to try and keep things neat.

"Oh? What, like *Mass Effect Three*? That's my game. James Vega kicks ass. He should be in charge of the team, not Commander Shepard."

Gibson was further confused as Max took his time organising the sheet and bed cover, throwing it on, then straightening it out carefully before fluffing the pillows. The man was a contrast to say the least. A slob in one way, and completely nitpicky another.

Gibson stifled a yawn. "The Shepard fans will kill you if they hear you say that. Mine's also third-person RPG but it's a bit different to *Mass Effect*. My guys are all assassins. The concept is a superhero squad with drag queens, gays and lesbians." He slid into the bed, wincing at the lumpiness of the mattress, and snuggled in under the duvet with a sigh of relief at being warmer. The flat was chilly. Max watched him, a faint smile on his face.

"Sounds riveting. I'd play it." He watched Gibson squirming to get comfy. "I know it's a crap bed," he murmured as he turned off the table lamp and slid in beside him. "One day I'll be able to afford a better one."

Gibson face-planted into his pillow. "Uh-huh," he said sleepily. Post-orgasmic doze was setting in. "You have to have something to aspire to, I guess."

A pair of soft lips pressed against his hair and Gibson smiled.

This is nice. I don't stay over at a guy's place ever. What does this mean?

"'Night, Gibson. Sleep tight." The bed rocked as Max got settled and Gibson shuffled back so he was the little spoon.

An arm draped over his waist and warm breath huffed against his shoulder. "'Night,"

Gibson murmured. "Thanks for letting me stay."

Soft lips kissed his shoulder. "Thanks for staying," was the whispered reply. "Now go to sleep."

"'Kay." And with that one last word, Gibson fell asleep.

Chapter 6

The ringing of his phone and its loud rendition of Madonna's 'Like a Virgin' took Maxwell out of a dream featuring him, Gibson and a bowl of cream and catapulted him into the early morning. The warm body wrapped around his was incentive enough not to answer and let it go to voice mail.

Something hard pressed against his stomach and Maxwell wanted to take the tour to discover what it might be. He pushed a strand of fair hair off Gibson's face, his heart clenching at the sight of Gibson's sleeping visage, long eyelashes against pale cheeks and lips that were slightly opened. The man sleeping beside him was beautiful. A quick peek under the covers confirmed Maxwell's suspicions—yep, one lovely, cut pink cock currently prodded him, attached to a lean, tight little body that Maxwell wanted to touch, hold and never let go. The little piercing in Gibson's belly button winked at him, inviting his mouth to taste it.

Maxwell clapped a hand against his forehead as he lay back, picking up his phone to see who had called.

"You knew this was a bad idea, arsehole," he muttered to himself. "He told you he doesn't do commitments but no, you had to take him home. And now you want to keep him."

The phone call had been from his boss, Grant. Maxwell had a horrible feeling he was going to be asked to cut short his days off and take over someone's flight. He wasn't happy to do that when he had Gibson in his bed so he declined to check his voice mail yet. It was only nine am after all. Grant could go fuck himself if he thought Maxwell was getting up earlier to go to work. Although he could use the money the extra shift would bring. Maybe then he could buy a new damned bed.

Last night had been memorable. And the 'not fucking?' Maxwell didn't think he had it in him to be inside this man and not want to own him and have his metaphorical babies. It was a level of intimacy that with anyone else might be a fuck, but with Gibson would seem to be much more. Maxwell couldn't explain it, and it pissed him off. He had no idea why he was so invested. It had been best to not go that far.

Gibson snuffled and pressed himself closer. Maxwell took a deep breath. His own morning woody was getting stiffer by the minute with the feel of the insistent press against his belly. Gibson blinked and then unfocused green eyes looked into his.

"Morning." Like a kitten, Gibson stretched and gave a deep moan of pleasure as the kinks in his body straightened out.

Maxwell wanted to moan but for an entirely different reason. "Morning." He cleared his throat because his word had come out sounding like he smoked a pack of cigarettes a day.

"I heard the phone. Do you need me to go home?" Gibson sat up, the covers pooling around his waist. Maxwell's eyes were drawn to his tight nipples and morning woody.

"No, no rush. It's my boss. I'll phone him in a little while." He needed to get out of bed. Now. Before he lunged at Gibson and pinned him down, slid inside him with all the lust and need in his being and lost his soul to a forest-eyed pixie with a belly bar.

Maxwell swung his legs out of bed and stood up. He found his underwear on the floor, slid into it and was better equipped to face the day.

"I like your tattoo," Gibson murmured as he squinted, sat back against the couch and stretched. "I know you don't like talking about it but it's awesome. Maybe I should get one," he mused thoughtfully. "A dragon, or a phoenix or something. Right here." He drew back the covers, turned onto his stomach and waved a hand at his arse. "On the small of my back. What do you think?"

Maxwell was still trying to process the round backside with its tempting pucker perched high in the air, looking as perfect as an arse could be. He cleared his throat again.

"I think it's a personal decision. I only have the one tattoo, and I wouldn't get any more. I think your skin is perfect the way it is. But, yeah, a dragon might look good if that's what you wanted. I'm going to go shower. I won't be long then you can do the same if you want."

Maxwell made his way into the tiny bathroom off his lounge-cum-bedroom-cum-kitchen and closed the door. It contained the rudimentary items, including a bath with a shower. He started the water running and pulled the faded blue curtain across. For the first time, the shabbiness of his flat hit him. As for his possessions spread all over the place, he liked to see them. Years of living on the streets and having to hide what little he'd had made him want to display them, know they were there as affirmation he'd got *stuff*. He'd never wanted to impress anyone before; no one he'd brought home had made him evaluate where he lived and what he had.

He stepped into the bath and picked up the soap as he began washing. A rush of air wafted through the room, making the curtain ripple. "Stop worrying about your place," he muttered. "It's better than sleeping in a fucking cardboard box. Better than scrounging in dumpsters trying to find food, sleeping in shop doorways or running away from guys who want to make you their bitch. You should be proud of what you have, Mooch. You made it here." He hated his street name but it reminded him of where he'd come from. He'd earned his name through his unfailing persistence trying to cajole shopkeepers and restaurant owners into giving him food that hadn't been thrown out. It had earned him a lot of slaps around the ear. He didn't want to think about the other things he'd done for food.

He finished washing, conditioned his hair, checked his pubes— he liked to keep them neat—and switched off the shower. He opened the curtain and stopped short at seeing a naked Gibson sitting on the toilet, his face pale, lips set.

"How long have you been there?" Maxwell stepped out of the shower onto the ragged bathmat and plucked a towel off the rail, wrapping it around his waist. He was glad now he hadn't beaten off in the shower. That could have been embarrassing.

"Long enough. I badly needed a pee so I didn't think you'd mind. You were so busy talking to yourself I don't think you heard me come in and take a leak." Gibson's eyes were shadowed. "You did sleep on the streets, didn't you?"

Maxwell took a smaller towel off the rail and dried his hair. A direct question deserved the direct answer. "Yes. For about eighteen months until I was sixteen. I was homeless and I lived wherever I could find a place to sleep." He'd only ever told this story to Oliver and even then not in much detail. Only the fact he'd been homeless for a while.

Gibson stared at the scorpion. "Is that when you got that?"

"No. I got it after."

"After what?"

Maxwell stared at Gibson in frustration. "After I got off the streets. To remind me." He wasn't going to say it had been done in memory of his dead boyfriend. Levi had had a fascination with scorpions.

Gibson's mouth opened and Maxwell knew he was about to ask 'remind him of what.' He huffed and rolled his eyes.

"To remind me I'm not the same person I was then. That I still carry a bite even though I might be different now, and life can still sting like a fucking scorpion."

That was the other reason for the tattoo. One he needed to remind him about where he'd come from.

"Oh." Gibson stood up. Maxwell's eyes were drawn to his semi-erect cock, the shaven groin, the pink balls hanging between his legs. There was the faint sheen down there where he'd missed a bit. Gibson was beautiful and damn sexy, and Maxwell's whole body ached with want.

Underneath the towel, he grew hard. He needed to get dressed. "Did you want to get in the shower? There's plenty of hot water still."

"Why were you on the streets in the first place?" Gibson wasn't giving up. Maxwell took a deep breath and hung the hair towel back on the rail.

"Because I ran away from the foster home I was in after I lost my family. I didn't like it. The boy I was friends with said we'd be better on the streets and I believed him. For a while, we were. He died and I was on my own."

Maxwell didn't want to think about the wasted body in their cardboard home. Holding the cold, dead body of your best friend and lover was a memory he tried to forget.

"God, Max. I'm so sorry." Gibson stroked his arm and stepped closer, his hand gripping Maxwell's arm.

Maxwell shrugged. "It was a long time ago. I got off the streets, went back to school and started over. I reinvented myself so I didn't end up like Levi."

"Levi was your friend's name?"

Maxwell nodded. "Yes. He was a bit older than me. He was a drug addict and it got the better of him."

Gibson nodded. "Was he your lover?" His green eyes searched Maxwell's face as his hand tightened.

Maxwell's throat clenched. "No." *Liar*. He wasn't sure why he'd lied about that bit. It was just too personal to admit yet. "Now can we leave this topic alone please? I'm not partial to bearing my soul so early in the morning. I haven't even had coffee yet."

Maxwell stormed out of the bathroom. He heard the shower start and heaved a sigh of relief. "God, he's a nosy little bastard." He pulled on a pair of grey sweatpants, a black tank top and went into the kitchen to put the kettle on for coffee. He had no idea how Gibson liked his—or if he even liked the stuff.

Fifteen minutes later Gibson came into the lounge, towel wrapped around his waist. He dropped it and started dressing in the clothes he'd had on the previous night. Those silver shorts slid over his pert butt and Maxwell averted his eyes. He was still half hard under his towel.

"Do you take sugar in your coffee?"

Gibson nodded. "One please. No milk, just black." The black mesh tee shirt was pulled over his head and he finger-dried his hair while Maxwell stirred the coffee.

"I'm sorry if I upset you," Gibson said as he put on his glasses and searched for his bag. "I wanted to know a bit more about you. I mean, you seem like this put-together guy—funny, cute, sexy—yet you lived rough. It's not what you'd expect."

Maxwell sighed as he came over and handed Gibson his mug. It looked like he wasn't going to get away with not telling his story. Perhaps he should get it over and done with.

"I worked hard to leave the old me—Mooch—behind. When Levi died I realised I didn't have to be on the streets anymore, so I went to a shelter. It so happened they'd been awarded a huge grant by this rich woman called Beryl Carnegie. She put a load of money into rescuing street kids. I was one of the lucky ones who managed to get help."

Gibson stared at him in wonder. "Wow, that's awesome. She must have been an incredible lady." He cupped his hands around the mug and took a sip of coffee.

Maxwell smiled sadly. "She was. Eighty years old and wanting to change the world. I met her a couple of times. She *was* awesome. That money paid for me to be checked out by a doctor, it paid to fix my teeth…they weren't good, because of my bad diet and the fact they'd been knocked out a couple of times. She even enrolled me in an evening class so I could finish my schooling."

"*Who* fucking knocked your teeth out?" Gibson said, tiger-cub fierce. Maxwell thought he looked adorable.

"Bullies, other street kids, gang members, take your pick. You were easy pickings if you were a street kid. Fair game for anyone. Including perverts and guys looking for a fuck or a blowjob." Maxwell shrugged. "You learnt to run, and you learnt to fight back. You pick up some tricks on how to stay safe and protect yourself."

His chest tightened. Those days had been dark, lonely and scary. Trying to stay out of the gangs who promised what looked like paradise—somewhere warm to sleep and food—yet wanted your life and soul in return, being asked to do unspeakable things…it hadn't been an easy life. But Maxwell had managed to rise above it. He'd done things he wasn't proud of, but he'd survived. And he had soul scars hidden under the bluster and bonhomie of Maxwell Lewis.

Gibson walked over to him and wrapped slim arms around him in a hug. "You're amazing," he whispered against Maxwell's ear. "I'm sorry you went through all that without any family around to help."

Maxwell closed his eyes, savouring the scent of soap and man even as the memories came flooding back and twisted his soul. Gibson made him want to share things. "My mum died in childbirth with me. I only had my dad and my older brother Kent and we were close." He hugged Gibson tighter. "They went on a trip to Switzerland in 2000 for the weekend. I was in school so couldn't make it. There was this huge mudslide in the Alpines and they were both killed."

Gibson made a small sound of distress. "Oh, God, that's awful. You went into foster care?"

Maxwell sighed. "Yeah. It wasn't that bad but Levi convinced me it was and we ran away. I was stupid. And by the time I realised the grass wasn't greener…" his voice tailed away "It was too late to go back. I couldn't do it. Couldn't leave Levi. He was my best friend. He needed me."

For a moment both men stood there in each other's arms and then Maxwell stepped back. There'd been enough emotional baggage unpacked. He needed caffeine.

"You want more coffee? I can use some more." He wandered to the kitchen and busied himself refreshing his cup. Gibson laid his mug down on the counter and watched Maxwell fill it up.

"What made you become a flight attendant?"

Maxwell stirred sugar into Gibson's drink. "I left school, worked various jobs, got a job in a travel agency. I loved seeing the other parts of the world. It was so far removed from where I'd been so I decided I wanted to see it too." He handed Gibson his mug. "I applied to the airline four years ago and got accepted. And here I am."

He plonked himself down on the still unmade bed-couch. "Now you know about me. What about you? Who is Gibson Henry?"

Gibson sat cross-legged on the bed as he sipped his coffee. "I'm perfectly ordinary. I design games, own a company with my best friend Jack, travel around meeting sexy flight attendants and blowing them in the loo." He grinned. "My parents are still alive and live near Edinburgh with my brother."

"And you never see the same man twice." Maxwell smiled at him but he didn't feel smiley. "And there's nothing ordinary about you."

Gibson flushed. "I'm a little commitment-phobic," he admitted. "I'm too young to settle down and I have a lot I want to do still. Jack and I want to finish designing *Camp Queen* so it can win the Croesus Gaming Award." His eyes gleamed with avarice. "It's a big award in the industry and if we get it, it could mean a lot of investment into the company so we can develop more games and grow. Perhaps even win a bigger award. We missed out on winning the Croesus with one of our previous games, *Blockshock*, when it was nominated. I want to win this time. It would be a real coup for an LGBT game to win it, and mean a lot to me personally too. It has to be the best it can be."

His face shone with hope and thoughts of obviously getting something that meant a lot to him. Maxwell hoped his dream would come true for him and one day he might get to see Gibson's expression if he actually won.

Maxwell's phone rang again, and with a pang of guilt, he realised he hadn't called Grant back yet. He answered and winced at the peeved voice of his boss.

"Thank you *so* much for answering your phone," the syrupy voice echoed down the line.

Maxwell rolled his eyes. "Sarcasm is wasted on me, you know that. I deflect it to something I can use, like, 'Oh do you remember you gave me time off and this happens to be my time-off day—one of three, if I'm not mistaken." He winked at Gibson. "Whaddya want?"

"Fiona has food poisoning. She can't make the late flight to Spain tonight unless we want her upchucking all over the passengers. I wondered if you wanted the shift and I'll make it up to you."

"Oh yeah? How?" Maxwell stood up, held the phone to his ear with his shoulder and stretched. He was gratified to see Gibson's eyes follow the movement of his tee shirt and fix on the treasure trail on his belly.

Yep. I've still got it. He wants me.

"You can still have your three days off, and you'll get a full day for the one shift tonight. That's a bargain."

In Grant terms, it was indeed a bargain. He was tight fisted with his 'in lieu' arrangements on holiday. "Okay. I'll be there later for the shift. Eight pm, yes?"

"Thanks Max." Grant sounded relieved. "I appreciate that. See you later then." He rang off and Maxwell threw his phone on the bed.

"Working tonight then?" Gibson asked. "That sucks."

Maxwell blew out his cheeks. "I could use the money, and I've nothing else planned so why not." He looked down at Gibson. "What are your plans for the weekend?"

"I've got work to do on the game today and Jack and I are going to a friend's house tonight for a get together. Tomorrow I'll be back working on *Camp Queen* again." He blew back a piece of hair that had fallen over his forehead. "More drawing. More coding. More fine tuning. It's a never-ending process but God, I love it."

The passion for his art clearly reflected on Gibson's face and envy pinged in Maxwell's chest. He loved his job, but not like this. Not with the overwhelming 'kick it to the curb' intensity showing in Gibson.

When he'd been a kid, all Maxwell had wanted to do when he grew up was be a doctor. He wanted to wear the white coat and heal people, make sure they didn't die from some stupid thing like amniotic fluid embolisms—the thing that had killed his mother when he'd been born. He knew it hadn't been his fault; his dad had told him over and over again he wasn't to blame in any way, but still. It hurt knowing his birth had killed her.

That chance had disappeared with the death of the rest of his family and instead, his path had gone a different route.

"Sounds cool. And you get to go to a party in between. Is Jack gay too?"

Gibson snorted loudly. "God, no. He's got a girlfriend, Beth. They're mad about each other. Jack and I have been buddies since secondary school." Gibson smiled fondly. "He's a bit like you, a white knight, but the straight version. Always fighting my corner and rescuing me from scrapes." His lips pursed adorably. "I seem to have a habit of getting them into them."

"And why do I believe that?" Maxwell murmured in amusement.

Gibson giggled and Maxwell fell even harder down the slippery slope of wanting to keep him. "Oh, God, I remember once this kid at school was picking on me because of my size. I mean I'm not saying I'm a lightweight or anything but I'm a computer geek for God's sake, not a fighter. Jack is a big guy. He's not fat but he's scary. We were always called Laurel and Hardy at school because of the size difference. Anyway, this guy punched me, a couple of times and Jack comes barrelling across the quadrant and punched his lights out. I swear the bullying dick flew a hundred feet through the air."

Maxwell's blood was boiling at the thought of anyone punching Gibson not once, but twice. "Jack sounds like a prince," he growled. "I'm glad you have someone like him looking out for you."

"Yeah, he's the best. He had a hernia though when he saw me in this outfit. He worries about me." Gibson smirked. "I'll cute 'em to death if anyone tried to mess with me." He leaned forward on his hands and knees and waggled his bum.

Maxwell's groin took notice of the sexy gesture and his pulse rate increased to land speed record. "Oh yes. On the scale of one to ten of cuteness, you overshoot the mark."

Gibson raised an eyebrow. "I have a tendency to do that. Overshoot." His peal of laughter made Maxwell snigger.

"God, you are incorrigible." Maxwell was getting more and more out of depth with this man. "Anyway, breakfast. Do you want some?"

Gibson shook his head in regret. "I can't. I need to get home, get on the laptop. My fingers are itchy to get some work done. Plus these damn shorts are cutting my balls in half so I need to change." He smiled up at Maxwell as he clambered off the bed. "Best I get off."

Gibson looked around the messy room, and spotted his coat. "I guess I should pop this on over the outfit so I don't get had up for indecent exposure. Or get beaten up or mugged. That wouldn't do. I'd have to call my crazy nut-kicking guy to help me out again." He chortled and as he shrugged into his coat, Maxwell's sense of loss grew stronger.

"Oh, okay. Well, thanks for last night and this morning. I enjoyed having you over."

Gibson grinned at him. "It was a pleasure. Thanks again for the whole *Karate Kid* thing at the club."

He picked up his bum bag and clipped around his waist. He reached out and framed Maxwell's face in warm hands as he kissed him. Maxwell closed his eyes and pretended, for one split second, that Gibson was his. He infused all the longing in his heart into the kiss and when they finally split apart, Gibson looked dazed.

"Great kiss. Whoever gets you one day will be one lucky guy." Those well-meaning yet careless words cut Maxwell to the quick.

He tried to smile. "Yep, one day he won't know what hit him."

Gibson flapped a hand. "Okay then. See ya around, Max. Thanks for having me."

Gibson was gone in a flash of blond hair and white teeth, leaving Maxwell with a heart emptier than it had ever been before. Gibson hadn't even bothered to give him his number. Maxwell scowled darkly. Even though he had it already, the implications rattled in his head like a loose marble. It was obvious Gibson had seen this as just a stray hook–up, and Maxwell was damned if he was going to beg for more from the man. He did have some pride left.

Chapter 7

Gibson wheeled his suitcase into his flat at midday, and heaved a sigh of relief at being home. The flight to Dublin had been an eventful one. Slotting his case in the corner of the hallway, with a promise to himself to unpack later, he went straight to the fridge and got out a beer. He opened it and took a large, thirsty swig.

"Christ, that was the flight from hell," he muttered grumpily as he slumped down at the kitchen breakfast nook on a stool. "I am never flying WeGo Air ever again."

"I don't know why you changed it in the first place, dumb arse." Jack wandered into the room, clad in sweatpants, scratching his belly and yawning. "I told you to stick with Target. They're far better." Jack yawned again and opened the fridge. He took out a half-empty bottle of orange juice and drank it down.

Gibson knew why he'd changed airlines but he wasn't going to tell Jack the real reason. Maxwell Lewis had been on his mind, creeping in like an insidious flame flicking at his heart, and he'd tried to ignore it. Cruz had noticed Gibson's man crush too and given him hell too about it. His fiery little friend had told him in no uncertain terms he was being a 'pathetic idiot' trying to avoid something his heart wanted, all uttered in Cruz' adorable Spanish accent. Gibson wasn't comfortable thinking of Max as something permanent.

"Change is good," Gibson said waspishly as he raised his beer to his lips and took another swallow. "Variety is the spice of life and all that crap."

"Yeah?" Jack grinned slyly. "It didn't have anything to do with you being hung up on that cute air steward guy you fucked then?" He sniggered as Gibson felt his face flush.

God, was he that transparent about his infatuation?

"I am so not *hung up* on him," Gibson snapped. "And we didn't fuck. He didn't want to." He heard the pique in his voice and too late he realised he'd played straight into Jack's hands. His friend was like a Venus flytrap, inviting the unaware into its inviting depths only to be devoured to the bone.

Jack nodded sagely, blue eyes twinkling. "Oh, God. The great Gibson Henry being turned down for a fuck. What *is* the world coming to?" He cackled loudly at Gibson's rude gesture. "Gib, you haven't stopped talking about Max this, Max that. Then you went all quiet, and next I knew you'd changed airlines. I knew something was up."

He walked past and ruffled and ruffled Gibson's hair, which earned Jack a glare. "He got under your skin. Admit it. Changing your flight was your way of saying you don't want to care about seeing him again when you do. You have a reputation to keep up, don't you?" His tone grew admiring. "I have to say, I've never seen you like this over one guy. He must be something else. And I want to shake his hand when I see him."

"Why?" Gibson narrowed his eyes and huffed. He thought not for the first time how well Jack knew him. He had indeed changed his flight so he didn't have to see the sultry and sexy Maxwell Lewis again. Like a dessert of something fluffy and light on the outside, but dark, spicy and tantalising when you bit into it, the man had pervaded his thoughts; those chocolate brown eyes and firm lips invading when they had no business doing so. Gibson still remembered the soft kiss pressed to his cheek in the nightclub, as if by doing it, Max could take the sting out of his slapped face and make it all better. Gibson wasn't used to such tenderness. It scared him and when he was scared, he ran.

"Because he stuck up for you and did his crazy karate thing. I want to see it." Jack's voice brought Gibson back to the present— he'd forgotten he'd even asked a question. He'd been too busy seeing a scorpion tattoo on lean haunches and the shadowed expression on Max's face when he'd talked about his past.

"Well, yeah, there was that," Gibson admitted

"And I want to meet the man who's got you all aflutter." Jack winked.

Gibson snorted. "I think you have me mixed up with someone else who actually gives a damn. You know me. I don't do repeats. Usually," he amended hastily, because he had with Max. *Damn.* And he wanted to do it again.

"You tell yourself that." Jack's knowing smile irked Gibson no end. He ignored his friend and polished off the rest of his beer. He'd had nothing to eat so it gave him a pleasant buzz.

"I'm going to shower and change then I'm going to get stuck into some work. And I'm not going to talk about him again, so there." Gibson did the adult thing and stuck his tongue out at Jack as he brushed past him to get to the bathroom. "We've got a game to get ready because next year, we're going to win the award. I don't need any permanent distractions."

Jack nodded sagely. "I hear you. Enjoy your shower." He smirked.

Gibson flounced past him, flinging his hair back as he passed. All this talk of Max had made him horny. The memory of their frenzied frotting and the feeling of Max's fingers in his arse as their cocks rubbed together was giving him a hard-on. The shower sounded like a safe place to take care of it, even if Jack knew what he was about to do.

When the water was warm enough and steam billowed out in opaque clouds into the spacious bathroom, Gibson ensured the door was locked and stepped into the glass enclosure. He loved the shower for both its size and the larger showerhead producing enough pressure to massage his head and shoulders to ease the tension in his body. There was also plenty of room to jerk off, and as he smoothed Imperial Leather shower gel all over his torso, he gave his cock a sly twist or two to get him started.

Closing his eyes, he recalled Max's lips taking his in a kiss, sparking heat in his groin; his fingers deep in his arse, finding that spot that sent shivers through him and made him plead for more. Gibson stroked his cock, fingers gripping tightly, making sure he slid his thumb over the heated head, causing him to gasp in pleasure. The warmth of the water and the fragranced steam assaulted his senses until he was dizzy with the need to come.

He lifted one leg onto the small ledge than ran on one side of the shower. As his hand tightened its grip on his dick, Gibson reached down and pushed a finger inside himself. The simple fact of having his arse filled, with the memories of Max's thrusts inside him, caused him to shudder as he worked himself faster, making one finger into two and holding back the needy groans as he synchronised his hands to both fuck himself and jerk off at the same time.

He lost his breath as water trickled into his open, panting mouth and when he finally peaked, he remembered Max's smouldering eyes gazing into his, watching him reach orgasm. Gibson's cock splattered its release onto wet tiles and was washed away.

62

Boneless, satiated and wondering what the hell was going on with him, Gibson finished his shower, turned off the water and wrapped a towel around his waist.

"I need to get a grip," he muttered to himself as he ran a razor over his barely-there stubble. Troubled green eyes looked at him from the mirror. "This guy is messing with my head and that's not on." He scowled at himself. "Maybe you need to get him out of your system by hooking up with someone else." There was the faint swelling of hope it could work. "I think later tonight I need to find me a club, dance and get laid. That'll solve the problem of Mr Maxwell bloody Lewis."

*****

Lying in a strange bed in a puddle of cooling semen and sweat twelve hours later, after a night of tequila and some fairly dirty dancing on the floor at The Capella Club, Gibson stared at the man snoring softly beside him. Vic had been sweet enough, blowing Gibson off in the bathroom then bringing him home to his small terraced house not far from the club, but the night hadn't been anything earth shattering. Yes, they'd fucked; Vic eager and willing to be nailed as much as Gibson had been to do the nailing. It had gotten them both off but Gibson had this feeling of something *unfinished.* As if it hadn't been enough to simply have a good time. He was a little uncomfortable about the fact that as Vic had been ploughing his arse, Gibson had been thinking about Phoenix's costume design. It happened often with him when he couldn't feel an emotional connection to the man he was in bed with, but he was pretty sure when he'd been with Max, the man had been the only thing on his mind.

After they'd both got their rocks off, Vic had smiled, said, "That was good," and fallen asleep. Gibson now lay beside him in the wet patch wondering whether to catch a few z's or piss off home now. He decided on the latter.

He slunk into the bathroom, did a superficial clean-up and got dressed. When he got back to the bedroom, which smelt of sex, cigarette smoke and sweat, he gathered up his satchel and left.

His flat was dark when he got home in the early hours of the morning.

Thank God I don't have an office job to go to. Being my own boss has its perks.

He wasn't tired so he decided he'd do some work on *Camp Queen.* He did some of his best thinking in the early hours. Getting back into the familiar tasks of sketching outlines and planning his scenes made Gibson forget everything other than the task in hand.

When he heard a cough behind him, he looked up to find Beth standing in a soft towelling robe and a wry grin on her round face. Gibson liked Beth; she was good to Jack, had a wicked sense of humour and was always willing to play *Blockshock* with him. He and Jack might have developed the game but it was still a lot of fun to play as a gamer. There were still Easter eggs in the game Jack had hidden that Gibson delighted in finding.

Beth shook her head. "Gibs, it's six-thirty in the morning. Have you even been to bed yet?"

Gibson squinted at her and then at the clock on the wall. "Fuck, is it? I got in early this morning and got a little sucked in." He stretched, easing the kinks in his spine. Behind his spectacles, his eyes stung.

Beth shook her head as she moved to the kitchen. "I guess you could use coffee then. Unless you're going to try and get some sleep now?"

Gibson yawned. "Coffee first, then sleep." He smiled at Beth gratefully. "Thanks."

"You look knackered." Beth remarked. "And you pong a bit too. Had a good night then?"

Gibson flapped a hand. "So-so. And yes, I'm aware I'm not as fresh as I could be. I'll shower in a sec. I need to get some caffeine inside me first then I'll crash."

Beth chuckled as she pottered in the kitchen. "You're the only guy I know who can go to sleep on caffeine and Red Bull. If it were me, I wouldn't be able to sleep at all."

She came over and passed Gibson a steaming cup of coffee. He took it thankfully.

"It's a gift." Gibson drank hot gulps of strong coffee. "It's what keeps me going so I can get all *this* done." He waved at 'this,' his laptop and various drafts of character sketches, ideas for scenes and half-crumpled balls of paper. "Creativity is a bitch."

"I heard you had a beau," Beth remarked, staring at him over the top of her coffee cup. "Jack told me you saw this guy and now you're stuck on him."

Gibson put his cup down on the side table. "Firstly, who the hell says 'beau' anymore?" he snorted. "And secondly, I am not hung up on anyone. It was a one-night stand and won't be repeated." He wondered why that thought triggered a pang in his chest. "Anyhoo, what does your gormless fellow know? He's nothing but a big galoomp."

Beth spat out a mouthful of coffee as she laughed. "I'll let you repeat that when he's awake, shall I? He'll probably give you a wedgie."

Gibson winced, remembering the last time he'd had his underwear driven up his crack by an unrepentant Jack. "He can try," he muttered. "But seriously, what is all the sudden concern with my love life and the men I see? Have I missed the camera crew for *My Mad, Sad Life* lurking around and am I on air all of a sudden?"

My Mad, Sad Life was a current reality TV show where hidden cameras recorded roommates living together and cataloguing their chats, antics and their sometimes sexual activity. Gibson had watched it once then vowed to never do it again.

"No, dufus. We're worried about you. I mean, you flit from guy to guy like a honeybee and I guess we want to see you settled."

Gibson rolled his eyes. "God save me from happy het couples who think they have to have their gay best friend as 'settled' as they are." His tone was affectionate, and Beth sniffed.

"This guy sounded like the real deal, though. I mean, he did the Crane Kick for you."

Gibson grinned. "He did, didn't he? And he was sweet afterwards. He's funny and sexy, and oh my God, his story about living on the streets made me want to hug him better, you know?" He broke off at Beth's knowing smirk, feeling his face heat up. "What's that for?"

"You liked him," she said dreamily. "Our little boy is growing up."

Gibson scowled. "Maybe I liked him better than any of the others. That doesn't mean I want to marry him." He sniffed regally.

Even if I do have this crazy desire to call him up and see how he is. I mean, what the hell? Since when did I become potential relationship material?

Beth giggled. "Oh, Gibson. I love you can pretend to be so damn clueless. It's so adorable."

Gibson threw the lounge cushion at her. "Bite me," he snarled. "Don't you have somewhere else to be rather than harassing me so early in the morning?"

Beth delivered her parting shot as picked up the other coffee mug, presumably Jack's, and made her way back to their room. "The very fact you get all angsty about me teasing you is enough for me. I think you have a thing for this man."

With a cheeky grin, she disappeared into the hallway. Gibson sat for a few minutes, finishing his coffee and trying uncomfortably to convince himself he did not have a thing for Max, and if he never saw the man again, it wouldn't matter one jot.

Two weeks later, after not being able to stop thinking about Maxwell bloody Lewis, and having a dry spell that was driving him crazy because the men he was with weren't doing it for him anymore, Gibson broke down and sent a text.

*****

Maxwell had given up on ever hearing from Gibson again. He hadn't seen him on any other flight he'd attended on since the club outing, but then he supposed Gibson wasn't some bigwig businessman who lived on aeroplanes as a second home. Also, Maxwell been working long hours and the opportunity to get together with anyone anyway had been lean. He'd even refused a blowjob in the loo a few days ago, when he'd done another flight to New York. Maxwell knew he was seriously messed up.

He was sitting with Leslie and Oliver in a bar in the middle of London when he got the text. At first Maxwell ignored it. They were deep in discussion about debating whether bare-backing was ever an option in porn scenes. Oliver ran to the belief that even if he knew the other guy's history and had his medical results shown to him to prove he was clean, he'd still not bare-back for a scene. Leslie agreed and in all truth, so did Maxwell. In his opinion, bare-backing in porn was never an option. But it was fun riling Oliver by playing devil's advocate and seeing him get all worked up about things. Since they were involved in a heated debate about the topic, he didn't want to spoil the fun by checking his texts.

Leslie shook his head, black bangs falling across his face. "I think it's two against one, Max." He grinned. "And I'm thirsty. I think we need more drinks. Come give me a hand, baby?" He cast a heated look at Oliver who cast one back.

Maxwell rolled his eyes. "We all know what that means. The two of you are going to go get off somewhere under the pretext of buying drinks. Fine, away with you. Don't be too damn long. I'm parched."

His friends stood up with alacrity and were soon halfway across the floor towards the bar—and no doubt the bathroom. Maxwell sighed as he took out his phone. He was feeling the loneliness tonight. That lonely feeling was assuaged somewhat when he saw the text message.

"Oh my God. Gibson," he murmured with growing excitement. His fingers scrabbled to open the message.

Gibson here. Hope you don't mind. Wanted to say hi.

Maxwell chuckled. *Hi. How are you?*

Ok. Wondered if you wanted to get together for a drink?

Maxwell couldn't type fast enough. This was encouraging.

Sure. When and where? I'm flying long haul this week. Back in town Monday.

Oh. I see.

Maxwell waited in anticipation for the next text. It was a long time coming.

I guess maybe we could do the Tues night? Do you know Galileo's Restaurant in Soho?

Yep. I'm with someone now who knows the owner. Want me to get us booked in?

Maxwell waited smugly. He could imagine sitting across a table from Gibson, with some fine wine, great food, candles on the table, as they stared into each other's eyes...

His romantic dream was somewhat shattered with Gibson's next text.

Oh only for drinks. Not dinner. That ok?

Maxwell scowled. Fine, if that's all he wanted, he could do that. Gibson obviously didn't see this as a 'dinner date.'

Sure. Say 8 pm then?

He was so fixated on watching his phone and waiting for the beep of a received text he didn't notice Oliver and Leslie arrive back at the table. His friend gave a low chuckle and gave him a hard punch to his arm.

Maxwell glared at him. "Stop bruising the merchandise." He glanced down at his phone. No reply.

"You had this look on your face like Santa had told you that you got that anatomically correct G.I. Joe with the nine-inch dick you always wanted." Oliver smirked. "Is there someone special on the other end of the phone?"

Leslie laughed softly and raised one immaculately plucked eyebrow in Maxwell's direction.

Maxwell flushed. "It's Gibson."

Oliver's eyes widened. "The geeky guy you're hung up on?"

Leslie slapped Oliver's arm with a snort. "Don't call him a geek. It's rude."

Oliver stared at him in confusion. "Why? It's what he is, isn't it?" He turned to Maxwell for confirmation.

Maxwell huffed. "Yes, he's a geek, but he's my geek and I'm the only one allowed to call him that. He asked me to drinks at Galileo's."

Leslie leaned forward, hand on Maxwell's arm. "Oh, I'll call Eddie, get him to ask Giddy to set you up a nice, quiet table somewhere where you guys can get to know each other. Anything special you want, tell me. I know Eddie does this fabulous beef dish—"

Maxwell leaned across and laid a finger across Leslie's lips. "Slow down, Patti Stanger. He doesn't want dinner, only drinks, so I guess we'll be sitting at the bar." He removed his finger.

Leslie looked dumbfounded. "Honestly?" he pouted. "That sucks."

Maxwell had to agree. But he'd take what he could get. "It's fine. At least he texted me." He smirked. "The boy's been thinking about me."

Oliver looked amused. "Maxwell, if I didn't know you better, I'd say you've not stopped thinking about him too. I never thought I'd see the day someone on your spreadsheet made a return entry."

He winked. "Apart from me of course. I think I rated four and a half in technique." The smirk on his face made Maxwell grin.

Leslie gave a soft snort. "Do you mind? I'm right here, hello." He mock-glared at Oliver, whose face fell.

"Oh hell, sorry beautiful. I meant, you know, when you weren't in the picture, not now of course." Oliver reached over and cupped Leslie's chin. "You know you're all the man I ever want."

If it hadn't been something Maxwell himself pined for, the look of adoration between two men would have made him barf right then and there at such sweetness.

Maxwell cleared his throat. "God, you two. Stop it. You're giving me a woody. I—"

His phone pinged and he hastened to check it.

Eight pm is fine. See you then.

Maxwell knew he was busted when he looked up to see both his friends staring at him in amazement. He immediately tried to lose the goofy grin he knew he wore. But it was too late.

"Did you see your face?" Leslie said breathily. "Oh-My-God. Our Maxwell is in L-O-V-E if my romance radar has anything to say about it."

Oliver nodded his head. "Oh yes. I saw it too. My friend, you have it bad." His slow glance was assessing and if anyone saw right through him at this moment, it was Oliver.

Maxwell shrugged. "So I like the guy. Sue me."

Oliver smiled. "I like this new Maxwell. It's about time you found someone special." He waved over a waiter. "Could we have a bottle of champagne please? I think we have a little something to celebrate. My friend here found out what his heart is for."

Maxwell sighed. He was *so* never going to live this down.

Chapter 8

Maxwell waited at the bar in Galileo's for Gibson to arrive. He looked at his watch. Seven fifty-five. He'd been sitting there close on half an hour, knocking back a beer and trying to look as if he wasn't anxiously waiting for his date to show.

He loved this restaurant. The ambience was welcoming, the staff professional and friendly, and the owner of the place wasn't half bad either.

Leslie gushed about his best friend Eddie and his partner Gideon Kent, and Maxwell had to say, Gideon was very easy on the eyes. He watched in day-dreamy lust as Gideon strode around the restaurant being all bossy and macho. A polite cough brought him back down to earth. Maxwell blinked and looked into amused green eyes framed with thin black spectacles. The glasses looked different to the ones he'd seen before and he wondered how many pairs Gibson actually had.

"Am I disturbing you?" Gibson asked drily, but his eyes were amused. "I can leave if you've seen something else you'd rather have."

Maxwell knew there was no one else he'd rather have than the sexy man standing in front of him. Gibson's hair shone like spun white gold. He wore tight black jeans, with a thick belt and buckle, a tight, dove-grey shirt with a darker grey collar and open cuffs to his forearms, and black boots. The man took Maxwell's breath away and did nothing to ease the ache in his cock, an anticipatory ache he'd had since getting to the venue. The appreciative look his drinks partner gave him as he ran his eyes down Maxwell's body made his trousers feel even tighter. Maxwell thought he rocked it dressed in butt-hugging camel chincs and a white button-down shirt teamed with his dark brown leather bomber jacket.

"God, no," Maxwell said breathlessly. "No one here could possibly have anyone better than what I'm looking at." Too late he realised that probably sounded a little presumptive but Gibson didn't seem to mind. His face beamed at the compliment and his pale skin went rosy.

"Thanks," he murmured as he struggled onto a high barstool. His feet barely touched the footrest and he scowled briefly. "They always make these damn things too high for people like me. Someone should tell them we're not all six-foot monster men."

"Shall I ask them for a booster step?" Maxwell laughed at the fierce glare directed at him. "Or not. It's good to see you."

"Yeah, you too." Gibson beckoned to the bar lady. "How was the flight? Where did you go?"

"I was in New York again. Had a layover, met some old friends and now I'm back on the shorter routes."

Gibson nodded. "Cool. What can I get you to drink?"

"I'll have a screwdriver, please." Maxwell watched as Gibson gave the order to the bar lady, including a Jack Daniel's for himself.

"Are those new glasses? I don't think I've seen them before." Maxwell peered at them.

Gibson shook his head. "Nah. I have five different pairs. I like to change the frames around depending on what I'm wearing."

"You don't do contacts then?"

Gibson frowned. "Can't abide them, they make my eyes water and I get too much eye strain, especially working on a computer all the time. I have this thing about my eyes—worry about losing my sight one day—so I try and keep them happy."

Maxwell was intrigued. "Where does that fear come from?"

Gibson shrugged. "I saw this film once when I was a kid about a guy going blind and since then it's been something I worry about." He made an adorable moue. "I know it's crazy. My optometrist says my eyes are healthy, but that's me."

Maxwell huffed. "Huh." The bartender put the drinks down on the bar and Maxwell picked his up. "I was surprised to get a text from you."

"Not as surprised as I was I sent it," was the quick reply. "Jack and Cruz have been pestering me ad nauseum to get in touch, and don't even let me get started on Jack's girlfriend Beth." He rolled his eyes but Maxwell did a double take when he saw the flush staining Gibson's cheeks.

"What?" Gibson said defensively. "I told you I don't do repeats, yet here I am. What does that tell you?"

"I don't know," Maxwell said honestly. "I'm not great at reading between lines. I prefer a full-on direct approach myself. Sounds like your friends forced into you something you don't want." His chest tightened at the thought.

Gibson's eyes darkened and he licked his lips as he glanced around the restaurant. "That's what you think? I make my own mind up, Max." He grinned. "A bit like this."

He reached over and pulled Maxwell's face to his, sliding his mouth over Maxwell's willing lips and kissing him hungrily with the skill of a porn star. Maxwell wasn't quite used to this sort of display in public, especially when it wasn't even in a gay bar. As his mouth was assaulted, all he could think of dreamily was, 'God, he's a great kisser.' When Gibson released him, he stared around in a dazed stupor. The bar lady was grinning widely, her face indicating her approval.

"Was that a bit more direct?" Gibson's mouth was swollen, probably much like his own. His face was pink, the hunger in his eyes unmistakeable.

Maxwell simply nodded, dumbfounded. "As long as we don't get kicked out," he finally squeaked.

Gibson grinned. "The guy who owns this place is gay, half his friends are gay and they often indulge in a little tonsil hockey themselves at the tables. I've been here and seen it and let me tell you, it's quite a show."

"Yes, I know Gideon is gay. I know most of his friends as well, but still, he might take exception to two guys swallowing each other's tongues in his place."

Gibson snorted softly. "Better than swallowing something else in public," he murmured. "I'm rather hoping that might come later though, in private."

"Oh, God," Maxwell said faintly. "You are the wicked poster child for the sexual frustration of men everywhere, I swear."

Gibson raised two fingers to his mouth, sucked on them a couple of times, drew them out with a pop then held them in front of his mouth like the smoking barrel of a revolver. He blew on them and Maxwell truly believed he might come in his pants.

"You know Gideon then?" Gibson sipped his drink, seeming to be unaware he'd caused grievous bodily harm to Maxwell, and yet the glint in his eyes and smirk on his face indicated otherwise. "I've been here a couple of times. He seems like a nice enough guy. Sexy too."

"Not personally, only by name and conversation. I know his partner Eddie's best friend, Leslie, and I used to sleep with *his* guy."

Gibson looked confused, so Maxwell elaborated. "Leslie is now going out with my ex-fuck buddy Oliver, although you probably know him better as Nicky Starr, the porn actor."

Gibson's eyes bugged out. "You used to fuck Nicky Starr? No way, José."

"Way." Maxwell sipped his drink, taking great delight in Gibson's astonishment. "Oliver and I go way back. Obviously we don't get together anymore that way, as friends."

"Oh fuck. That's hot. Thinking of you and him…" A shudder racked Gibson's body. "Is he as good in person as he is on camera?"

"Better," Maxwell said with a smug grin. "Oliver is inventive yet he cares about his partner."

Gibson took a deep slurp of his drink. "Sweet."

"Not to harp on it, but why *did* you call me?" Maxwell was harping on it. He couldn't help himself.

Gibson rolled his eyes and threw him an exasperated glance. "You're a bull terrier, you know that? Why can't you accept I'm here and let it be?"

Maxwell shrugged. Honesty was probably the best policy. "I've no desire to invest more of myself in someone who's playing me. It's not where I want to be. Either we see each other simply as friends and that's it, or if we sleep together sometimes, it becomes something that might become more. I know it's early days and I don't want to scare you off, but I am not being a notch on someone's bedpost. Not anymore."

Gibson was quiet and Maxell wondered if he'd come on too strong.

But he was the one who contacted me, and he knew how I felt about being casual. At worst, we can maybe stay friends without benefits. It'll be tough but I'd do it.

Gibson looked up from the silent contemplation of his half-empty drink. "I liked spending time with you. I don't usually have guys on my mind afterwards, but you, I do. I thought maybe we could get to know each other better, see where this goes." He grinned. "I'm not lying when I tell you I like you, I want you, and I hope mad, animal sex is on the cards."

Maxwell's tummy squirmed in pleasant anticipation. His dick liked the idea too.

"I'm *not* looking to move fast, get married, adopt kids and move into a house together." Gibson grimaced in distaste. His fingers played with a paper napkin on the bar. He looked nervous. "That's a deal breaker. But if you're happy to take a chance and be with me when you're not gadding about the world up high, and see what happens between us, then that's a plan."

"I'm not looking for that either," Maxwell murmured. He cleared his throat. "Let's be clear. We see each other—exclusively— as and when we can?" He held his breath as he waited for the reply.

Gibson blinked. "Exclusive?" His hands stopped their fidgeting.

Maxwell's heart sank. "Yes. I mean, that's kind of how I think dating works."

"Dating?" Gibson's hands started playing with the napkin again.

Maxwell was out of his depth now. What the hell did this guy want? "Isn't that what we're going to do? Date?"

Had he completely misread the situation and made a fool of himself?

He knocked back his drink and waved to the bartender. He needed another. Gibson Henry was hard work. He gestured to their drinks. "Could we have a repeat please?"

The soft snicker from beside him made him glance round. Gibson had a grin on his face, a twinkle in his eye, and Maxwell had the distinct feeling he was missing something.

"What are you laughing at?" he muttered crossly.

"You are so gullible." Gibson chuckled. "I was yanking your chain, sexy." His hand reached up and caressed Maxwell's cheek. "I might be a bit of a slut but when I agree to *see* a guy, I'm monogamous." His eyes flashed. "Let's not call it dating yet, though. That's a big word. Let's call it seeing each other."

The warmth flooding his body was like treacle flowing through his veins and Maxwell loved it. He could live with that. For a while.

"Bitch," he sniffed as he paid the bartender. "I think this is going to be a barrel of laughs, being with you."

Gibson's face shadowed. "I can't say how it will all turn out," he warned. "But I'm happy to take it day by day, let things develop slowly…"

Maxwell reached over and covered Gibson's hand with his. "That's all I need. My social life is crap at the best of times, with my shift patterns and days off. I'll warn you it might not be ideal."

"Meh. It'll be fine. I have so much work to do I can keep myself busy twenty-four hours a day, so we're in the same boat." Gibson quirked an eyebrow. "Now can we leave the shit behind and do some serious drinking? Are you flying tomorrow?"

Maxwell shook his head. "Day off. We can get as crazy as you want…"

The evening passed in a blur of drinking, conversation and laughter and by the time the pair left Galileo's to walk off some of the effects, Maxwell was horny, drunk and desperate to take Gibson home for the night. He wasn't sure though if that's what his 'date' had planned so he went with the flow. It was when they were walking—or rather staggering—past Soho Square Gardens that he had a thought.

He pulled Gibson against the railings and pointed him towards the park. "I've always wanted to make out in a public park," he whispered. "How 'bout you?"

Gibson squinted through fogged glasses at the darkness beyond. "I'm not sure," he said doubtfully. "Haven't they got security, park keepers or whatever? And isn't it locked up?"

Maxwell shook his swimming head. "Nothing we can't handle," he scoffed. "I'm used to sneaking into parks. I lived in them when I was on the streets, remember?" He'd meant it as a light-hearted remark, but the look of sympathy on Gibson's face made him kick himself.

He'd managed to sidestep all Gibson's veiled questions. Over drinks, the man had been like a puppy worrying a stuffed toy, trying to shake the stuffing out of it. Maxwell didn't want to tell his new shiny toy about the rotten, shaming things he'd done as a homeless youth.

"Don't look at me like that," Maxwell murmured. "Those days are gone. Now come on. I can give you a leg up over the railings, and then climb over myself. If we keep to the shadows no one will see us. There's this cool garden hut in the middle I'd like to show you."

Gibson looked unconvinced. "Can't we go back to your place?"

"Come, on, spoil sport. It'll be fun." Gibson hardly had time to protest before Maxwell knelt down on the path on all fours and gestured to Gibson to climb on his back. "Up you go, leg over and onto the other side." He smirked. "Be careful of your crown jewels. I don't want them getting damaged before I've had a chance to have them in my mouth."

"Oh God," Gibson whispered as he clambered onto Maxwell's crouching form. "This is such a bad idea. I'm not used to this sort of physical activity—oomph. Fuck." The dull sound of a body hitting the ground had Maxwell standing up and peering over the fence.

"Gibson, are you okay?"

There was a rustling and an annoyed voice muttered, "Yeah, I lost my balance and fell over the fence. Tell me again this was a good idea?"

Maxwell hopped nimbly over, clearing the top with inches to spare between his groin and the spiked railing. "It was a good idea. Are you okay?"

Gibson was sucking on his hand, his face scrunched up. "No. I tore my damn hand on some bush or something. I'm injured. Carry on without me, Captain. I'll stay behind."

Maxwell laughed softly. "Give it here. Let me see."

He took Gibson's hand and peered at it. There was a nasty gash on the side of his hand, oozing blood. Maxwell reached into his back pocket and drew out a handkerchief. He wet it with spit and then applied it to the cut.

Gibson's mouth gaped open. "You carry a handkerchief? And then spit on it? What are you, my dad?"

Maxwell frowned as he dabbed at the blood. "You don't? And please, girlfriend. Enough of the dad comments. Not conducive to making out."

Gibson sniggered as he pushed his glasses up with one finger. "Maybe I have a daddy fixation."

Maxwell stopped what he was doing and stared at Gibson. "I can be your daddy," he said huskily. "Is that what you wanted to hear?"

Gibson swallowed. "Not really, but when you say it—wow. It does sound sexy."

Maxwell grinned in the darkness as he finished his doctor duties. The cut had stopped bleeding. "There you go. I'll take another look at it when we get home—mmphh."

His words were muffled by lips finding his as Gibson's tongue slid into his mouth while the Lacoste Red-scented bundle of warm man dragged Maxwell by the shirt and pulled him closer. The handkerchief was dropped to the ground as his hands found Gibson's hips. Hardness pressed against the lower part of Maxwell's groin and he gasped with need into the mouth currently excavating his with enthusiasm.

"You drive me crazy," Gibson groaned in between kissing the crap out of him. "I love the feeling of your stubble against my skin. I don't know what it is about you that makes me feel this way. You've been in my damn head for weeks."

"I know exactly what it is about you," Maxwell managed to get out. "You're as sexy as fuck. And ditto on the head games."

Gibson's husky chuckle turned Maxwell on more and he hefted Gibson up. Slim, strong legs wrapped around his hips as Gibson rocked against him, climbed him and attacked his mouth with renewed fervour. It took some doing avoiding knocking Gibson's glasses off his face but with some practice, and some creative angling, they found out how to manage it without injury.

A bang from the street brought them both to their senses and they jumped, unlocking their mouths.

"What was that?" Gibson whispered, tightening his clutch around Maxwell's neck, his dick pressing against Maxwell's harder than before.

"Probably a car backfiring," Maxwell managed to gasp out in between heaving breaths. "We need to get out of sight of the road. I thought we'd make out a bit, not go into full-flown grinding the minute we got in here." He plucked Gibson away from him reluctantly. Gibson got his feet back on the ground.

"Come with me." Maxwell took Gibson's hand and together they walked quickly towards the old black-and-white building in the middle of the park. "Let's stand under here. It's dark, more private than where we were and hopefully no one can see us." He cast a quick glance around the park. He could hear voices coming from the far side of the park, but they didn't sound close enough to be a problem.

"You know we could have gone back to your place or mine." Gibson's fingers idly traced a path down Maxwell's chest, and for the first time, looking down at Gibson's lazy finger, Maxwell noticed his shirt was half undone. The touch of Gibson's fingers against his bare skin inflamed his senses and Maxwell drew in a deep breath.

"I know. But I've never made out in a park, and it was on my bucket list, and I want to do it with you."

Gibson's smile lit up the darkness. "*You* are a romantic, Maxwell Lewis. A big soft romantic." This kiss was softer, sweeter and Maxwell thought his legs were going to buckle beneath him. All he could do was hold Gibson, kiss him back with all the feeling he had in his soul and fall deeper into the silky web being spun around him by Gibson Henry.

Maxwell knew he was in the middle of busy London, where city noises—backfiring cars, house alarms, trundling buses, people's conversation—were paramount, yet all he could hear was the rushing in his ears and the singing in his heart as he held the man in his arms.

I am in so much trouble with this one. God help me.

Gibson finally stopped causing mayhem on Maxwell's mind and body and stepped back, face flushed, bee-stung lips wet and a look of desire on his face.

"I don't want our first real time to be in a public park." Gibson huffed and adjusted himself. "Can we go home and get into a bed? I'm pretty sticky in my underwear already."

Maxwell found his voice. "Of course, sure. Uhmm, your place or mine?"

Gibson considered. "We can go to mine if you like. Jack will probably be there but he's cool when I bring guys home."

"You do that a lot then?" Maxwell cleared his throat. "I mean, I can't judge, I've had a bit of a revolving door in my place myself."

Gibson's face was unreadable. "There've been a few. Do you want the actual number?" His voice was even.

Maxwell shook his head, panicking he'd stuffed things up. "No, of course not. Doesn't matter. Let's go to your place, then. We'll get a taxi because it's quite a trek from here back to…" his voice trailed off as he realised he *knew* where Gibson lived but didn't want him to know he knew. That information had not been gainfully come by and he didn't want to admit he'd stalked him using the passenger manifest.

"Canning Town," Gibson offered helpfully and Maxwell smiled. *Result.*

He glanced at his watch. "It's still early enough to get a taxi. Come on, let's go."

They slipped quietly along the path towards the exit and once again, Maxwell got down on his knees and Gibson once again went over, this time with no injury.

By the time they stepped out of the taxi and into the rather swanky flat Gibson and Jack shared—Maxwell admitted it was a cut above his messy place—there was a sense of awkwardness between them. The passion was still there; the sexual tension in the taxi on the drive over had been unbearable, but entering the quiet of the flat, and Gibson taking his hand and guiding him to what Maxwell presumed was his bedroom was too much like other times a man had led Maxwell to a sexual encounter.

One that hadn't meant as much to him.

Maxwell wanted this to be different.

He stopped outside Gibson's bedroom and the other man turned to him with a question in his eyes. "Are you okay? Did you change your mind?"

Maxwell shook his head. "No, of course not. I don't know what the hell's wrong with me. I guess I'm nervous?" His insides *were* jellied.

Gibson chuckled. "Nervous? Don't be daft. What is there to be nervous about?" He opened his door and beckoned Maxwell in. Gibson closed the door, switched on a bedside light, and Maxwell looked around, admiring the room, trying to get himself back in sync.

"This is trendy. Very you. Cool and classic. I especially like the picture of the muscly dude in leather and the chick in Lycra. Are they from your game—?"

Gibson reached over a soft finger and pressed it against Maxwell's lips. "Yes they are. Now shut up. You're blabbering. I think someone needs to get their clothes off." He grinned and started tugging at Maxwell's trousers.

Maxwell reached a hand down and grasped Gibson, stopping him. "Wait."

Gibson blew a strand of hair from his forehead, his expression uncertain. "What? You *are* having second thoughts, aren't you? Maybe we should have gone to your place."

Maxwell shook his head. "No, not that. Just…"

He removed Gibson's glasses, setting them down on the nearest surface, and pulled him closer, gripping his tight, round arse in hungry hands. He took his mouth in a kiss. *That* was better, he thought happily. Kissing Gibson was his favourite thing to do. The stirrings in his chinos bore testament to the fact.

Gibson moaned softly into his mouth, a sound that made Maxwell's skin prickle with heat and his cock perk up from its semi-hard state to full flagpole.

"It's not that I don't want you," Maxwell murmured in between sloppy, hot kisses. "I want you too much. I was in danger of flaring out, like the Human Torch."

"Hmmm." Gibson's tongue licked Maxwell's top lip. "I can feel how hot you are. Can I take your clothes off now? Cool you down?"

"Be my guest." Maxwell had already started pulling Gibson's shirt over his head and at the sight of pert little nipples and a smooth, toned chest he closed his eyes and imagined he was in heaven.

The impatient removal of clothes led to a few chuckles, soft sighs and breaths of awe as each man revealed the other. By the time they were both naked, any reservations Maxwell had disappeared, and it was all he could do not to jump on top of Gibson and slide into home base. His eyes ran greedily over the now supine man on the top of the bed, lying with arms raised above his head, legs splayed apart wantonly, cheeks flushed and eyes hooded with desire.

For him.

"God, Gibson," he whispered. "You are one gorgeous man."

Gibson's long, swollen cock laid against his belly as he stroked himself lazily, a sly smile on his face indicating he had no doubt as to what he was doing to Maxwell. Gibson's mouth was reddened, his cheeks pink where Maxwell's goatee had rubbed his pale skin.

"So are you. Come over here. I want you in my mouth and I need to taste that scorpion. I want to you to fuck me so hard I lose my breath." He frowned. "We are doing that tonight I take it?"

Maxwell nodded, the sight on the bed stealing his breath. "Definitely."

He crawled onto the bed, straddling Gibson's thighs then bent down to take more kisses from the sweet, willing mouth seeking his. Their cocks pressed together, skin met skin, heated and damp, and Maxwell held Gibson's hands above his head as Maxwell plundered a hot, wet cavern of tongue and lips.

Gibson ground against him, pushing his hips upwards and making soft, breathy noises. His scent stole into Maxwell's nostrils like fragranced steam in a sauna. Gibson pulled away his mouth, leaving Maxwell needy and disappointed.

"Come up here," Gibson gasped as he tugged at Maxwell's hips. "I want what you have. Feed it to me."

Maxwell needed no urging and he scooted up to straddle Gibson's chest, still holding his wrists prisoner, and then slowly, teasingly, painted his lips with the wet tip of his cock. Gibson's mouth opened as he tried to take him in. Each time Maxwell moved back, until a deep, unhappy growl from his lover made his spine tingle.

"Stop teasing me, arsehole." Gibson's body writhed beneath Maxwell's. "I need you." The plea was cut off as Maxwell pushed himself in between those swollen, pink lips and Gibson smiled around him as he took Maxwell in. His eyes closed in bliss and Maxwell could only watch in hunger and a sense of awe as his most sensitive part disappeared in and out of Gibson's talented lips.

He tried not to thrust too deep, not wanting to take liberties, but when Gibson did one particularly deep suck, causing his cheeks to hollow, Maxwell cried out, letting go of Gibson's wrists and flattening his hands against the wall instead. Gibson obviously had no qualms about Maxwell fucking his mouth; his now free hands immediately gripped Maxwell's hips and began pulling him forward, taking him deeper and deeper until Maxwell could take no ore. He wanted to come inside Gibson.

He uttered a throaty growl and pulled out, looking down at a wild-eyed, spunk-smeared Gibson as he panted and recovered his breath.

"Where's your lube and condoms?" Maxwell managed to say.

Gibson reached under the pillow next to him and shoved a tube and a condom into Maxwell's hand. Maxwell's hands trembled as he sheathed himself. The lube he opened, rubbing it over his dick, wincing as he did so because he knew the slightest touch was going to set him off.

"Do you want me on my knees?" Gibson panted. "I don't mind how you take me."

"I want you face to face." Maxwell pushed Gibson's legs apart and dribbled the lube over his hole. "I need to kiss you while I'm in you."

As he prepared the wriggling, moaning man beneath him, both kissing and twisting fingers inside him, Maxwell acknowledged this was the closest he'd been emotionally to another man. Gibson was everything he'd ever wanted.

"Enough prep already," Gibson gasped. "Do me, for God's sake."

Sliding inside a tight, heated channel, hearing Gibson's cries of both pain and pleasure, feeling his muscles tighten around him as Maxwell gained momentum and thrust in a paroxysm of want and lust—it was as if Maxwell had been waiting for this moment all his life.

For this intimate act, with this man.

Maxwell struggled to control himself from coming too soon, and he damped down the rising emotions in his body making him want to blurt out stupid things too soon. Cheesy, sentimental things like, 'I want to keep you forever. Please don't ever go away.' And, 'I think I've been waiting for you all my life.'

The dual act of fucking Gibson's mouth with his tongue and being inside him was almost more than Maxwell could bear. The smell of sex permeating the room together with the smell of sweat, the sound of their flesh slapping together and the overwhelming pleasure in his groin—Maxwell fell long and hard when he came, jettisoning into the condom with a strangled grunt. A prickling sensation flooded his skin, and there was an exquisite tightness in his groin and backside as he clenched muscles already aching from his exertion.

Gibson gave a soft cry as Maxwell collapsed on top of him and his hand moved faster as he pleasured himself, something he'd been busy doing while Maxwell was ploughing into him.

"No, let me," Maxwell gasped as he pushed those frantic hands away. He slid down and sucked Gibson's pretty cock in, sucking hard and teasing his balls and taint as he did so. Gibson's hands clenched the sheets as he muttered expletives and curses and entreaties for Maxwell to finish him, take him deep.

When Gibson cried out he was close, Maxwell moved off and watched as Gibson's spunk covered Maxwell's belly and chest. When Gibson was spent, Maxwell licked his cock clean, and then crawled up to lie beside his lover.

The two men lay replete in silence for a while, both getting their breath back. Maxwell turned to lie on his side and watch Gibson, who looked as if he was dozing. Maxwell wasn't sure what to do next. Was he expected to stay? Should he leave? He knew they'd agreed to date but how far was that being taken?

"I feel you watching me," Gibson murmured, opening his eyes. His hand came out to gently caress Maxwell's sweaty chest. "You're wondering what happens next, aren't you?"

He turned on his side to face Maxwell. Gibson's face softened. "We crawl under the covers and get some sleep," he whispered. "In the morning, maybe I'll get to taste your scorpion like I wanted to. We can go to breakfast at this little roadside cafe down the road makes the best hash browns. Then maybe we can come back here and *I* can fuck *you*." He swung his legs off the bed and stood up, motioning to Maxwell to do the same. Gibson drew back the duvet, wrinkling his nose at the mess on the top then motioned to Maxwell to get back in bed. Once they were both in, he drew the cover over them both and snuggled into Maxwell's side, resting his head in the crook of his shoulder.

"This okay?" he asked sleepily.

Maxwell couldn't answer. The simple and unexpected pleasure of having Gibson's warm body snuggled next to him like a warm puppy was playing havoc with his vocal chords. Instead, he tightened his arm around him, placed a soft kiss on the blond hair tickling his nose and settled into sleep.

Chapter 9

"Sooooo…" Then "Soooo," even louder again. Finally, "Hey, dick breath!"

Gibson looked up in irritation from his workstation to see Jack staring at him, contemplation on his face. "What? You realise you interrupted me at a critical moment when I'm drawing? What the hell is so important?" He had a bit of headache and wasn't in the best of moods.

"When do I get to meet Maxwell?" Jack leaned back in his chair, closed his laptop and slid his feet onto his desk. He slid a piece of gum into his mouth and chewed.

Gibson's temper flared. "You interrupt me to ask me that? Jack, what the hell is wrong with you?"

Jack chewed noisily, knowing how much it annoyed Gibson. His friend had a thing for pushing him lately on the subject of Max. "I want to meet the guy," Jack whined, then popped a bubble. "I mean, you've been seeing him ages now and I still haven't met the dude." He squinted fiercely. "Has the tiny Spaniard met him yet? Because, if he has, I'm challenging him to a duel. I'm your *best* best friend so I get to see this Maxwell dude first."

Gibson rolled his eyes and huffed out a breath. "No, Cruz hasn't met him. He only saw him at the club the night we met. But he and Craig have gone to South America now on a backpacking trip and I have no idea when they'll return. Some sort of sabbatical," he said gloomily. He missed Cruz but they texted every now and then when Cruz remembered to keep in touch.

"And the reason you haven't seen Max yet is because we normally come here when you're flat-out asleep in bed, and you don't get up until like, eleven o'clock in the morning, and by then he's gone. And his work roster is crazy so to be honest, I haven't even seen him much either." Gibson scowled, remembering their last fight about that specific subject.

He and Max were into their fifth week of 'seeing each other' and in that time, they'd probably been together less than the number of fingers he had.

Jack chuckled. "Oh yeah, I remember the fight you two had on the phone. You were like a little spitting kitten. Very entertaining to watch, I have to say."

Gibson grinned wryly. Yes, it had caused one bitch of an argument when Gibson had pitched a hissy fit. Gibson hadn't thought he was getting as many happy times as he should with a dedicated 'boyfriend' and it had royally pissed him off. He enjoyed his alone time, but in all honesty, he'd come to depend on Max's solid presence, his warmth and humour and his sexy body. He never thought he'd have admitted that fact. The matter had resolved itself a few days later after they'd realised they were both being wankers. The make-up sex had been awesome.

Gibson had even managed to meet Oliver Brown and his spitfire of a boyfriend Leslie a couple of times. Gibson had been awestruck at the thought of meeting *the* Nicky Starr. He'd hardly been able to get a word out, and been so tongue tied that Leslie had roared with laughter and whispered to him that Oliver was just an ordinary man, and to 'breathe, honey, breathe.'

"Where is Maxwell today then?" Jack popped another bubble.

Gibson gritted his teeth, wanting to poke his eye out with his shading pencil. "Probably up over the sea, somewhere," he muttered. "Flirting with a passenger."

He'd heard all about the stories of Max's past airline antics—the layovers with call boys on tap for discreet hotel visits, the quick shags in toilets and blowjobs in the less-populated sections of the aircraft. Gibson had even seen Max's *Sexcella* worksheet. He'd been playing a game on Max's laptop, seen the sheet, and with no respect for his man's privacy, he'd taken a peek. He'd been amused at what he'd found.

When Max had found Gibson ogling over the varying attributes of the men he'd slept with over the years, he'd quickly shut it down and moaned at him for his invasion of privacy while hastily telling him there'd been no additions since meeting Gibson.

Max's ire hadn't lasted long; honestly, all Gibson had to do was kiss him to shut him up and he was a goner. Gibson smirked at the fact he *did* have the power. And when he licked long slow trails down Max's scorpion tattoo…it drove the man crazy with lust.

"Dirty little bugger," Jack chuckled. "What are you thinking about with that look on your face?"

Gibson waved his pencil. "None of your beeswax." He hunched over his laptop, back in the land of *Camp Queen* and Phoenix.

"Sooo…"

Gibson hurled his box of paperclips at Jack on the other side of the room—it was a small room, only big enough for the two desks—and swore, "Hell, Jack, what now?"

Jack blew another gum bubble as he frowned. "You have this nasty little imp temper," he mused. "You look all sweet and tiny but inside you're nothing but an itsy, bitsy demon child."

Despite his impatience at his friend's interruptions, Gibson's mouth curved in an unwilling smile. Max had said much the same thing last week when Gibson had chucked a pair of highlighters at him. Max had made the comment about Gibson being like a cupcake with vanilla icing: sweet and pretty. Gibson thought it had emasculated him so he'd tossed his stationery. After the highlighter had hit Max on the cheek, Gibson had been relegated to being a spicy devil cake with a forked tongue. He preferred that description.

"Beth wants to cook dinner for us all here," Jack said with an injured tone. "Maybe you can ask Mr High Flyer when he's available for it."

Gibson sighed. "Fine, I'll ask him when I see him. He's flying out tonight and only back the day after. He has a layover in Venice."

No doubt he'd be getting pictures of the city, together with pictures of Max's dick, and no doubt there'd be some hot and heavy phone sex later. It was how they kept each other going. Max had suggested a Skype session, something apparently his friend Oliver and partner Leslie did regularly, but Gibson wasn't too sure about it.

"Is that it then?" he asked testily. "Can I get on with my work now without you *so*-ing in my ear every couple of minutes?"

Jack waved airily. "That's it. I wanted a plan to meet the guy who has tamed my Gib."

Gibson turned a frosty stare on Jack. "He has *so* not tamed me, arsehole."

Oh yes he has. Admit it. He's become special to me in a way I never thought I'd see.

Gibson's mobile rang. He smiled when he saw who it was. "Mum. Hi, how are things at home?"

His mother sighed. "Hi, darling. Things are okay here. Your dad still isn't feeling too well; he's going for more tests. Ricky is fine and Haggis says hello."

Haggis was the old family dog, a mix of cute and clever mixed with collie and a bit of Dalmatian. "I'm sorry about Dad. Do you want me to come home? Is there anything I can do?" Part of him wanted to go home and see his workaholic father and tell him to take it easy, and part of him hoped his mother would say no, because he did have a load of deadlines to meet on his gaming efforts.

"No son, that's not necessary." Doris Henry sounded tired and Gibson wondered if he should go home anyway. "Ricky's here, he pops in every night, so we'll be fine. We're seeing you in next month anyway for your niece's birthday, aren't we?"

Richard's adorable daughter Chloe was turning six years old at the start of September, and was the apple of both her father and uncle's eye. "Yes, I'm flying up early in the morning. I'll get a taxi to you." Max was scheduled to be on the flight, spending the night in Edinburgh. Neither of had them had talked about him going to meet Gibson's family. Gibson hadn't offered and Max hadn't pushed.

His mother laughed. "Well, that'll be fine. Dad's sleeping at the moment or I'd let him say hi. But he's been tired so best let him catch a snooze when he can."

"Okay, Mum. Give him my love when he wakes up. Ask him to give me a ring and we can have a father-son convo."

Doris snorted. "Convo? Is that text or game speak, Gibson? I assume you mean a conversation."

Gibson rolled his eyes at Jack. He did love his mother but she was a stickler for proper speech. "Yes, I mean a conversation."

Jack was grinning at him across the room, no doubt realising what was going on. As the favourite best friend, he too had been subjected to a few ear bashings on the proper use of language.

"Anyway, the reason I called, other than to see how my youngest son was faring, was to ask you to please bring that old Hibernian FC scarf your dad left at your place last time we visited. He swears blind he had it recently and he won't accept he didn't. He's got this bee in his bonnet about wearing it to a match in a few weeks' time."

Gibson nodded. The scarf was balled up in his cupboard somewhere—at least he hoped it was. A sudden trickle of panic set in. He hadn't seen it in a while. "Sure, I'll bring it. I can't wait to see you both again. And my gorgeous niece of course."

"Good, I'm looking forward to seeing you too, son. I'd better get off, Haggis wants walking and he's going crazy. Say hi to Jack for me and his lovely girlfriend." She paused. "Should I be saying hello to anyone special in your life, Gibson? I mean, I know you don't do relationships as such, I can't remember the last time I actually heard you talk about the same man twice. And your friend Jamie has been popping around here asking after you. He still seems very keen."

"Mum, please." Gibson was mortified at the fact his mother knew he was a player. Jamie had been a guy he'd hooked up with on his last few visits to Cramond—gay pickings were slim in the small village—but he'd been clear to Jamie that the last time had been it. Jamie had started getting a little possessive and Gibson had needed to cut him loose. Thank God Gibson had never given him his mobile number or he'd have been flooded with texts and entreating phone calls.

"Actually, there is a guy I've been involved with for a while. His name is Max, and he's cabin crew on the plane I'll be flying in on."

"Ooh." His mother's voice perked up. "Well, you'll have to bring him to visit when you're here. I'd like to meet the man who has your attention longer than a week. Right, got to go. Talk to you later." His mother rang off and Gibson put his phone down with a defeated sigh.

"Crap. Now she wants to meet him. Why didn't I keep quiet?"

Jack cocked an eyebrow. "You didn't keep quiet because you wanted to tell her that her baby boy wasn't a slut and actually had a man in his life who he didn't pick up at a club for a quickie."

"Fuck you." Gibson heaved another sigh. "I'll find some excuse not to take him. Tell them Max had to work an emergency shift or something."

Jack shifted in his chair, his face puzzled. "Why not introduce him to them? What's the harm?"

Gibson hummed. "It's complicated. I mean, this whole thing with him has moved quite fast and it's different. I like Max, a lot, but I'm not sure I want him to meet my family yet. That seems"—he struggled to find the right word—"so permanent. We're having a great time together and it's fab having a regular guy to go out with so far, but it's like chalk and cheese for me from where I was to here. I don't want to move too fast and find we don't work out after all. And he's away such a lot and that's not going to change."

I miss him when he's not around. There, I actually admitted it.

Jack nodded. "I understand, but he's good for you, Gibson. I've never seen you so settled. Or happy, bro."

Gibson blew air out of pursed lips. "Maybe I'm not ready to settle down if I don't want to take him home yet?"

Fuck. Why the hell had he said that? He *was* happy. He cared about Max and the word 'boyfriend' had *nearly* slipped out of his mouth a couple of times when he was talking about him to others, but it was all a bit scary. He'd never done the relationship thing— what if he messed it up? And he'd have his folks all over his case because once they met Max, they'd love him. Anyone would. Gibson didn't want to disappoint anyone if all fell apart.

A noise at the door made them both turn towards it. His heart sank when he saw a pale-faced Max standing there in his cabin crew uniform and a bag slung over his shoulder. His face was pinched, his eyes flat.

"Max. I thought you were going to Venice?" Gibson's mouth was dry and he wondered how much Max had heard. Judging from his body language, it had been most of it.

Max moved into the room. "The flight was cancelled. Air traffic control problem. I thought I'd surprise you." His voice was tight as he nodded at Jack. "You must be Jack. Good to meet you at last. Sorry I came in unannounced. The front door wasn't locked."

Jack nodded, glancing from Max to Gibson. "Yeah, nice to meet you too at last. I was going out to pick up my girlfriend, so I'd better be off." He hefted himself off his chair and hunted around his desk for his wallet. "Gib, I'll see you later, yeah?"

Gibson swallowed past the lump in his throat and nodded. "Sure." He knew Beth was still working so Jack wasn't going to pick her up. He was giving him and Max space. He watched as Jack case a sympathetic glance at him and left the office.

"How much did you hear?" Gibson stood up and walked over to Max, who stepped back. Gibson's chest ached.

"From when you put the phone down." Max was still. "I'm sorry you feel that way. You should have told me."

"Max—" Gibson moved again towards his lover and Max shook his head.

"No, this isn't one of those times when you can kiss me and make me forget stuff, Gibson. I know your tricks and it only works when I want it to." The hurt on his face was palpable. "I'm sorry if I moved too fast, and again, I'm sorry I'm away such a lot. We've been through this and I thought we'd agreed to see how things pan out over the next few months."

Gibson wanted to hug Max, drive the bleak expression from his face. He opened his mouth to speak but Max beat him to it. "The trouble is, I'm more invested in this whole relationship than you. And after overhearing what I did… I knew it could happen, so honestly," he shrugged, "it's not that much of a surprise."

Gibson wasn't going to let his observation pass unchallenged. "Max, hear me out," he said firmly. "You have to understand where I was coming from. This is my first time in a real relationship and I'm scared I'm going to mess it up. And with you being away a lot, it's tough. I miss you."

Max's eyes shadowed. "Is that true?" he said quietly. "'Cos it didn't sound like it to me. It sounded like you doubt whether we should be together."

Gibson's stomach clenched. "I do bloody miss you, all the time. I get caught up in my work, but then I have a break and I remember you're not around to talk to, because you're thousands of feet in the air and I can't even text you and tell you because I know you won't see it until later and honestly, then the moment's kinda gone. I get all insecure and say stupid things like what you heard. I'm sorry."

Max still hadn't put his bag down and looked ready to run out of the door at any moment. Gibson wasn't going to let that happen. He moved closer to his lover and wrenched the bag from his hand, ignoring Max's startled look. He wrapped arms around his lover's stiff frame and buried his face in his neck. Max smelt of sweat, aftershave, curry and his own unique scent of Max.

"I'm glad you're here, honest. I like being with you. And may I tell you how damn sexy you look in your uniform?"

A soft rumble in Max's chest told Gibson he was thawing. He'd heard the same low chuckle when they lay in bed together, Gibson's ear against Max's warm body.

"And it's not that I don't *want* you to meet my family," Gibson murmured. "It's if they meet you, they'll love you, because who wouldn't, and if things go wrong, I'll never live it down and they'll make my life a misery for driving my first real relationship guy away—"

Warm lips shut him up and as he responded to the kiss, Gibson was relieved Max was still there, glad Max had understood his reservations and hadn't flown like one of his planes.

When Max finally released his lips, they stood together quietly. Gibson's nose wrinkled and he looked up into brown eyes. "Why do you smell of curry?"

"I had one before coming over here, it was pretty spicy. Sorry." Max heaved a sigh then moved to the kitchen to pour himself a glass of water. He filled the glass and turned to look at Gibson.

"Did you mean it when you said you're not ready to settle down? I won't be mad, so tell me the truth." His lips twisted in a painful smile. "Despite my high ideals about having a regular guy to see, I don't mind taking what I can get of you, whatever you want to give. It's better than not having any of you at all."

Gibson's heart tore a little at the precise moment he heard those humbling words. It looked like he'd done what he'd so not wanted to do: stuff things up. He needed to fix this.

He picked up his phone and dialled a number. Max stared at him in puzzlement.

"Gibson?" His mother sounded surprised.

"Hey Mum. I wanted to let you know Max, my *steady boyfriend*," he made sure to emphasize those words, "*will* be joining us at Chloe's birthday and he'll be staying over. We'll stay in my old room—together, if that's okay. I didn't think you'd mind."

His mother's squeal made him wince. "Oh, Gibson, that's wonderful. I can't wait to meet him. I'll get the room sorted in time, and make sure there are supplies."

A twinge of unease swept through Gibson. "What do you mean 'supplies?'"

"Well, the whole safe sex thing is important darling. I know how it is. I did the same thing for Richard when he had girlfriends to stay."

Gibson was mortified. "Mum, please say you're not going to do what I think you are. Truly. Dying here."

Doris Henry tut-tutted. "Now, Gibson, don't be coy. I'm an open-minded woman. Listen, sweetheart, I'm late for bingo. The taxi is waiting. I'll call you later in the week and see how things are going. I'm so excited to see you both." She laughed. "Oh dear, poor Jamie's going to be devastated."

The line went dead.

Gibson put down his phone and groaned. "Oh my God. My mother slays me. She wants to buy us 'supplies.'"

Max raised one eyebrow. He looked a little happier than when he'd first walked in. "You mean—"

Gibson nodded miserably. "Yes. I see condoms and lube making an appearance in my old bedside drawer." Max's snort made Gibson grin. "My mother is going to make sure she gets to know everything about you. Be afraid. Be very afraid."

Max regarded him with uncertain eyes. "I'm going to a birthday party? As your *boyfriend*?"

Gibson panicked. "Oh, crap, I guess I should have asked you first and not assumed…"

"It's fine. As long as you're sure about it all." Max's face looked happier but still unsure.

Gibson moved forward and cupped Max's cheek. "I'm sure. I've never taken anyone home before… so it means you're special. I'm sorry I fucked up and hurt you." He kissed Max's jaw softly. "Did I tell you how sexy you look in the uniform?" He stepped back, appraising Max with a leer.

Max grinned. "You did. I'm even better out of it though." He frowned a little. "Jack calls you *Gib*?" He winced as if the sound hurt him.

Gibson grinned. "He's done it forever. It's just his thing."

Max sniffed. "Not *my* thing. It sounds like some sort of hideous monkey name."

Gibson sniggered. "That's a gibbon you're thinking of, dummy."

Max pulled him close "Whatever it is, you're my Gibson. I promise to always use your full name, unless of course I'm in the throes of passion and I call you something else. Like sexy stud-muffin."

Gibson nodded slowly. "I can live with that. Now are we going to get busy here or not?"

Gibson pushed aside his personal deadline to get some stuff over to Everett to check. Making out and making up with Max right now was far more important.

Chapter 10

Maxwell woke with a start, heart pounding and with a dry mouth. His head was foggy and aching and he needed desperately to pee. He climbed out of his lonely bed; he hadn't seen Gibson for awhile. He'd only been back half a day from the last three days' non-stop flight roster, taking on more hours to get a couple of extra days off. He shuffled to the bathroom and winced when he saw the sight that greeted him in the mirror.

His hair was in disarray, looking as if someone had taken a teasing comb to it. It stuck up all around his face, which was pale, and fuck, was that a spot? Maxwell peered through unfocused eyes at the beginnings of the blemish on his chin. His eyes looked hollow and there were dark shadows under them.

In truth, he'd not been feeling well for the past few days and the last flight to Madrid had done a number on him. It had been hectic, filled with needy, crotchety passengers, a lot of them blindingly ill and flu-like even as they tried to hide it, and he had a feeling he'd caught something off the kid in seat 18D. The child had been runny-nosed, whining and had actually sneezed in Maxwell's face when he leaned down to take his food tray away.

Maxwell's chest ached, feeling tight, and he was still struggling to breathe. He relieved himself, sloped back to bed and huddled, shivering, under the covers. He couldn't sleep; ten minutes later, he was kicking the blankets off, burning up. He gazed blearily around for his mobile then remembered it was in the lounge. He couldn't be bothered to get up and get it. He wanted to call Gibson but he didn't have the energy.

"I need to hear his voice," he mumbled as he buried back under the covers. "He'll make me feel all better…" He coughed, his chest racked with pain and he held a hand to it, willing the spell to finish. When he could finally draw a breath, he lay there, exhausted.

This sickness reminded him of one of the times he'd gotten ill on the streets. Now at least he was in a bed with access to modern medicine. Maxwell didn't have much in his cupboards because he was hardly ever sick, and he didn't keep his medicine chest stocked up because he hated taking drugs, hence why he felt so shit now.

Back then, it had only been him and Levi; Levi feeding him water as Maxwell hacked up what was left of his lungs into a dirty piece of linen that had once been a restaurant cloth napkin. Neither of them had eaten for days, Maxwell too sick and Levi scared to leave him alone in case he died while he was gone.

"You never thought of me, though, when you died, you bastard," Maxwell was delirious in a haze of fever and remaining vestiges of a long-held grief. "You made me find your cold, dead body stuffed with the crap you fed into your veins." He remembered that part of his life as if it had only just happened.

He'd crawled into the corner of the doorway recess and lifted Levi's head onto his lap as he stroked greasy hair and the cold planes of Levi's face. Levi had been his world since Maxwell had been fourteen and yes, when they'd run away together he'd been legally underage for the sixteen-year-old Levi, but that hadn't mattered to either of them. They'd been all each other had and Levi had taught him what sex was, and about caring.

He sensed a comforting presence in his room, feeling a shadow falling over him and he smiled, imagining it was his Gibson here, watching over him. Dream Gibson took hold of his heart and stroked it softly, comforting him.

"I did some terrible things on the streets for money, Gibson," Maxwell whispered as he drifted in and out of reality. "I don't want to tell you about them, because you'd hate me. I'm not proud of them but they're part of me. And I lied to you." Feverish whispers echoed in the still room as tears trickled out of his swollen eyes. "I told you Levi was only a friend. But he wasn't. He was much more than that."

Soft hands stroked his hair. "I know, baby," Gibson whispered, his voice choked.

Maxwell tried to focus on the blurred figure sitting on the side of bed. "Gibson? I'm hallucinating, aren't I?"

Something foul tasting was forced into his mouth, medicinal and disgusting. "Drink this, it'll help break your fever," was the soft reply. "I'm going to get some washcloths and try and get your temperature down. You're burning up." Warm fingers brushed away the tears on his cheek.

Maxwell smiled dreamily. Everything was all right now. Gibson was here even if he wasn't. "I like this dream," he murmured as he fell into sleep. "And I think I love you." He snorted in laughter. "No, I *know* I love you. Don't tell the real Gibson, Dream Gibson, because I don't want to scare him away."

There was the sound of a soft gasp then a light kiss was pressed to his sweating brow. He revelled in the touch.

"Sleep now," came the whisper. "I'll be here when you wake up."

"'Kay," Maxwell muttered sleepily. "Please don't go away. I don't want you to leave."

"I'm not going anywhere," Dream Gibson said. "I need you to get better. Go to sleep."

Maxwell fell into slumber with the vision of his boyfriend, his blond halo of hair shining in the dimness of the room and green eyes looking down at him with some indefinable emotion.

*****

When Maxwell woke again, it was to daylight streaming into the room through half-open curtains. He blinked and struggled up to peer around him. The bedside table was cluttered with medicines and face towels and—was that a humidifier blowing steam into the air? He stared at it in bemusement. He didn't own a humidifier. The machine hissed and billowed scented clouds of eucalyptus. The time on his Lego Darth Maul clock said one pm.

"I must have been further gone than I thought," he croaked. His chest didn't feel as congested so he imagined whatever he'd been doing in his fever-driven haze had worked. He looked at the humidifier again. "Huh, even in a stupor, I'm the man."

"I doubt that," was the dry retort and Maxwell gave himself whiplash turning his head to see Gibson standing in the bedroom doorway, shoulder resting against the jamb, arms folded across his chest. When Maxwell's chest constricted this time it wasn't because he had some dreaded disease. The joy flaring through his body like strands of lightning filled it with emotion and flooded his senses.

"Gibson? When did you get here?"

Gibson came into the room and checked the humidifier water level. He added a couple more drops of oil to the heated water and swore as it spilled over onto his fingers. "About three days ago." He wrinkled his nose, wiped his hands absently on his jeans and stretched. His tee shirt rose above his waist to reveal a faint treasure trail and toned tummy. The belly bar wasn't there and Maxwell was disappointed.

Maxwell's jaw dropped. "Three days ago? I don't remember seeing you. Was this all your doing then?" He waved a hand at the bedside table and his happily steaming appliance.

Gibson nodded. "You've had a bad bout of bronchitis. I got stuff from the pharmacy, borrowed the humidifier from Jack's girlfriend Beth—he dropped it off for me—and I kept forcing medicine down you. You had nothing in your medicine cupboard." He cast an accusing stare at Maxwell. "I mean *nothing,* apart from a couple of expired condoms, an old empty tube of lube, a broken thermometer and a shower cap." He grinned. "With ducks on it."

Maxwell's face flushed beet red. "Sometimes I don't want my hair to get wet when I'm showering. Wet hair on the flight isn't something the passengers want to see."

"Yeah but ducks? Little yellow-lello ducks?" Gibson's face shone with mirth. "You must look so cute. I was tempted to put it on while you slept and take a picture. Jack was all for it too. He wanted to share it on Facebook."

Maxwell gasped. "You didn't, did you? Because that would be the height of cruelty…"

Gibson sat down on the bed and reached out and brushed sweaty hair from Maxwell's forehead. "No, I didn't. And I threw out the old condoms and crap. Hope you don't mind. I didn't want you taking risks."

"You fed me medicines? I hate taking that stuff. That's why I don't have it at home. What did you give me?"

"It was only paracetamol and some Day Nurse. You needed to break your fever, Max."

Maxwell narrowed his eyes. "You've been here all the time? Did I say anything stupid when I was so out of it?"

Gibson's eyes darkened. "Nah, nothing. Do you feel better?"

Maxwell might have just woken up but he wasn't stupid. He *had* said something, obviously, from the quick change of subject and the wary look on Gibson's face. But for the life of him he could hardly recall anything of the last three days apart from some memories of Levi still lingering in his brain and a vague recollection of Dream Gibson being in the room.

"I smell rank otherwise I'd hug you and give you a kiss for looking after me," he said. "I don't believe you've been here three days and done all this." He gestured at the room. "Thanks."

Gibson shrugged. "That's what boyfriends are for. I took the ravish key and opened up." He grinned. The 'ravish key' was the spare key Maxwell kept hidden in a secret place outside his front door in case Gibson got the yen to come over and 'ravish' him in the middle of the night. It was a fantasy of Maxwell's and not one Gibson had played into yet although he hoped one day it would come to fruition. "I brought my laptop over and worked when you were sleeping. The joys of being my own boss and being able to work from anywhere."

"Crap. I don't suppose I called work to tell them I was ill."

"No, I did. I remember you mentioned Grant was your boss so I found his number in your phone and called him. He said get better and don't come back until you're well because he can't have you spreading the germs to the passengers and crew. Nice guy though. He was worried about you."

Maxwell frowned. "You found his name in my phone? It's password protected."

Gibson rolled his eyes. "It's swipe protected and honestly, an L swipe to unlock? It took me two tries and I was in."

Maxwell narrowed his eyes. "You're a bloody computer hacker." He grinned. "Can you top up my bank account for me?"

Gibson sighed. "I'm not a hacker. Not much anyway. A ten-year-old could get in your phone. You're not the most security conscious of people, babe. Remember I got into your *Sexcella* sheet? The unprotected one, which should have some sort of password on it, given what was in there. I mean, a man's dick size is personal *and* confidential information." He shivered theatrically and cast Maxwell a sly glance.

A frisson of discomfort slid down Maxwell's spine. "You looked at it again?" He realised Gibson had called him 'babe' a moment ago and it threw his train of thought. He liked the endearment. He thought Gibson might have called him it before but his memory was fuzzy.

Gibson glared at him. "No, idiot. You asked me not to, didn't you? I don't break my promises." His beautiful lips curled in a kitten snarl and Maxwell wanted to kiss him. For being there when he'd been sick, for taking care of him like no else ever had since Levi had died, for being the best boyfriend a man could be. But he could taste his own breath and he had no desire to inflict it upon Gibson.

"Let me get up, have a shower and brush my teeth then I can apologise properly to you for that remark," Maxwell promised and was gratified when Gibson's face creased in a smile.

"Fine. Be careful when you stand up. Last time I took you to the loo you nearly fell down."

Maxwell blinked. "What? You've been taking me to the toilet?" He started to hyperventilate. "Fuck, how embarrassing. For what, number ones, number twos? Oh crap, this is bad."

By now Gibson was giggling and Maxwell's heart reached out and sucked the man deeper into it than he thought possible.

"Crass, Max. No number twos. I did have to hold it while you peed because you couldn't see straight and I didn't fancy cleaning piss off the walls." His face grew thoughtful. "You might need to take a laxative. You haven't *been* since I got here. But then you've hardly been eating anything other than those energy drinks I've been giving you. And soup."

Maxwell stared at him, face flaming, horrified at the talk of his potentially non-performing bowels.

Gibson cracked up. "Oh my God, your face. It's a perfectly natural thing, you know."

Maxwell huffed haughtily. "Not in my book. That kind of talk gets relegated to conversations about lady 'things' blocking up the toilet and eyeless dolls roaming homes looking for someone to kill. I don't like either of them." He swung his legs out of bed, feeling lightheaded. "Whoa. I see what you mean. You might have to help me to the bathroom."

Gibson helped him stand up and together they made their way to the shower. Gibson made Maxwell sit on the closed lid of the toilet while he brushed his teeth over the basin, then got the shower started, removed Maxwell's boxers and helped him in over the side of the bath. Maxwell's legs were wobbly, and his head a little fuzzy, but the sound of the water, its heat and the spicy smell of the shower gel as Gibson poured copious amounts over his shoulders was heaven.

"There," Gibson said huskily, watching as Maxwell massaged his scalp with shampoo and water. "I'll leave you to it. I bought fresh clothes and put them on the basin. Let me know if you need anything." He moved to draw the shower curtain and Maxwell reached out a wet hand and gripped his hand.

"You can join me if you like. Make sure I don't slip and fall down. That would be the boy-friendly thing to do."

He watched desire flash in Gibson's eyes as he bit his bottom lip. "I don't know, you've not been well, maybe you shouldn't overdo it."

Maxwell growled. "Gibson, get your clothes off and get in here right now. I'm strong enough to do what I want to do to you." He stroked himself softly and watched Gibson's pupils dilate.

His lover swiftly shrugged off his tee shirt, slid his jeans down over his hips, together with his tight blue briefs and stepped into the shower. Water cascaded over them both in the enclosed space as Maxwell drew the curtain.

"That's better," he murmured as he pulled Gibson to him, his lover's head fitting perfectly under his chin. Maxwell slid his hands down Gibson's flanks, pressing their groins together. "Right where you belong."

The soft groan leaving Gibson's lips was taken by Maxwell's mouth. Gibson tasted like spice and apple and Maxwell couldn't get enough.

"Why do you taste so good?" he managed between frantic, long, open-mouthed kisses.

"It's spicy chai tea," Gibson murmured as his hand caressed Maxwell's cock, teasing strokes threatening to blow Maxwell's mind. "Now shut up and kiss me."

To Maxwell, the slow, intimate sexual ballet taking place in a bathtub behind a faded shower curtain was worthy of a scene not out of a porn movie, but rather one of those sensual avant-garde films he'd watched in the past. He'd seen a few and never failed to get turned on by the slow, sensuous grinds of bodies against each other, tongues flicking softly then eating each other's mouths with groins and cocks pressing together, slick skin against skin as two men made love slowly, lovingly as droplets of water caressed eager bodies.

He wished he had a film camera in here, so he could play it back because he was sure the sinuous strokes of Gibson's firm torso against his and his hands encircling both of their cocks as he stroked them off was worthy of another watch…and another. His lover may

have smaller hands than him but he knew how to use them to bring
Maxwell to the peak.

When he finally cried out into Gibson's open mouth, his body
convulsing with pleasure and skin tingling with sensory overload as
he orgasmed, he took satisfaction in seeing Gibson doing the same.
Their combined essences dripped down bellies and legs to be washed
away in the water. The two men stood together, panting and replete,
Gibson's slick wet head pressed into Maxwell's shoulder as his
hands gripped Maxwell's arse, pulling him closer.

"That was what I needed," Maxwell gasped as he brushed wet
hair from his eyes. "*You* were all I needed to feel better."

Gibson was quiet and Maxwell looked down at him. "You
okay?"

His lover stood back, taking some shower gel to wash off the
remains of their release from his body. "Yes, fine." He sounded a
little uncertain. "You were something. I like it when we go slowly."
His hands reached up and cupped Maxwell's cheeks. "Now we
should get washed up and get out of here. You need to eat something,
get your strength back for another one of these." He waved down in
between their now clean bodies and grinned as he stepped out of the
shower and took a towel off the rack. He wrapped it around his waist
and left the bathroom.

Maxwell stayed where he was and shaved. Then, water wrinkled
and feeling like a new man, he got dressed and went to find Gibson.
He had something on his mind and Maxwell was determined to find
out what.

He found Gibson on the couch, computer on his lap, surrounded
by sketchpads, crumpled wads of paper in one neat pile at the foot of
the couch and a coffee cup—one of the three Maxwell owned. An
open container of Chinese food and what looked like the remains of
three packs of sandwiches were stacked neatly side by side on the
small side table.

Maxwell waved at the tidy debris. "This is what kept you going
while you were here?" Something different caught his eye and he
gasped. "You cleaned up some of my stuff."

Some of his worldly possessions had either disappeared, or been
packed neatly in piles on the rickety dining room table. Horror of
horrors, they might even be stored in cupboards.

Gibson looked guilty. "Sorry. I can't work in chaos, so I tidied up a bit. I'll mess it up again before I go, I promise." He cast a jaded eye around the now mostly empty room. "Although I have to say it looks better like this. I also threw out the dead plants."

Maxwell opened his mouth then shut it again. "What? But they might have lived, gone through a birth of re-growth!"

Gibson shook his head in amusement "Max, they were dead. D-E-A-D. There was no coming back for those poor critters. Best to let them go in peace and with some dignity."

Maxwell huffed. "I guess I'm lucky I didn't have a fish. Poor thing might have found itself flushed down the toilet."

He'd meant it as a joke but Gibson's face shadowed. "I'm sorry if I overstepped the mark. I was trying to help."

Maxwell's stomach clenched. "No, I was joking. I don't mind at all. God, I'm crap at this whole thing. My excuse is I was at death's door and I'm still recovering." He'd haul his stuff out when Gibson left.

He knelt down beside Gibson and peered at his laptop. "Whatcha doin'?" His fingers traced slow circles on Gibson's leg.

"I'm doing some animation." Gibson's eyes lit up eagerly. "I've got Phoenix how I want him, I think, and now I'm playing around with movements and simulations."

Maxwell stared at the complicated mess on the screen. It looked hellishly complicated to him but as he watched Gibson's slim fingers fly over his keyboard, creating incredible actions on screen, he was awed.

"Wow, you're a clever little fella, aren't you? That is awesome."

Gibson beamed. "I love it. I also do a lot of the design for the backgrounds and the environments." His tongue stuck out the corner of his mouth as the rather stylish figure on screen—Maxwell presumed it was Phoenix—leapt over what looked like a sleeping toad princess on the ground then performed a double somersault.

"What the hell is the thing lying down?" Maxwell muttered as he peered at the screen.

Gibson smirked. "*She s* called Rhea Lipstick. She's a drag queen with a nasty temper. You don't want to wake her up. She'll literally cut your balls off."

Maxwell gaped. "Hell, you're making up Mrs Bobbitt games here?" He clutched his testicles in sympathy.

Gibson snickered. "Feeling a little tender, Max?" He reached out and brushed Maxwell's crotch.

Maxwell wanted to purr in pleasure. "Keep that up and I'll make sure you're *more* than a little tender," he murmured.

Gibson grinned. "Promises, promises," he murmured, then went back to his game.

"What is the plan then with *Camp Queen*? How long do you think it will take you to finish it? You said something once about entering it into some competition?" Maxwell watched as Gibson blew a strand from his face and frowned.

"We've been working on this for the best part of two years, using every resource we have to help, and I'm hoping we have it finished by Christmas, for launch in about February next year. We might get entered in the Quasar or Gaymz Choice competition this year if someone nominates us. Then submissions for the Croesus Gaming Award take place next year in May." He scowled. "We missed the Quasar win this year by a couple of points...we came second. Which was good, don't get me wrong, but I want to be first."

"What do you get if you win?" Maxwell asked, fascinated. This was a side of a business he'd never thought about before. To him, the games were simply there to be played.

His lover smiled. "Monetary value-wise it's not great. Winner gets 5,000 pounds." Maxwell thought that was a damn good amount in his estimation. He could do a lot with that kind of money.

Gibson's eyes gleamed. "But the year after we launch, we want to enter the British Academy Game Awards. That's going to be the big one. And winning the Croesus next year will give us some respectability." He sighed. "The current games we have going bring in enough money for Jack and me to run our business and pay for the development of the new games." He looked uncomfortable. "Jack put quite a bit of money into Anomaly when we started up and he's virtually paid back but I want him back where he started.

"We're neither of us rich, but we earn a salary and the revenues pay for our flat and living expenses. Winning a big award will give us the boost we need to fund other games, pay for the freelancers we use and allow us to run the company." He grimaced. "I don't even want to think about not making it and having to go back to a nine-to-five job selling suit shirts or burgers. I'm over all that having–a–boss shit."

Maxwell had spent his entire life managing every single penny he earned to best advantage. He lived on a diet of canned food, soups, noodles, one-pound ready meals and didn't smoke or drink unless he was out socialising. Cabin crew wasn't the best-paid job in the world, although it had other perks. To him, being able to work where you lived and answer to no one sounded like a dream. A pipe dream for him though. He couldn't write, draw, was not musical and although he wasn't bad on the technology side—being able to fix things and understand how they worked—he had no transferable skills he could use to start his own business. He was a little in awe of Gibson and his obvious intelligence and creativity.

"How did you get into doing this anyway?" He watched as Gibson's fingers did miraculous things to the character on his screen.

Gibson didn't answer for a while and Maxwell sat patiently. He knew first-hand how his lover got so absorbed in what he was doing to the exclusion of everything else—even him. Gibson was entranced, busily typing something into one of the online forums he was always chatting in. Something to do with networking and problem-solving.

He stroked Gibson's thigh, but it still didn't seem to detract his boyfriend from his steadfast concentration. Maxwell sighed, a deep, heavy sigh echoing in the room. When it didn't get the reaction he wanted, he did it again, squeezing Gibson's leg tightly. This time Gibson glanced at him.

"Sorry, did you say something?"

Maxwell wanted to roll his eyes but refrained. "I asked how you got into this line of work."

Gibson shrugged. "I've been doing it since I was a kid. I was a geek at school and did all the computer science and IT things I possibly could. When I left school, I took a gap year, worked here and there then did a BA Hons in game design for three years in Manchester. Jack and I started Anomaly Media while we were at uni together and it evolved to what it is now."

"You lived in Manchester? Where, at the university?"

Gibson shook his head, brow furrowed as he studied something back on his screen. "No, we lived in Manchester not far from the University. I didn't need uni digs, and I was able to live at home. Mum and Dad paid my tuition so I didn't have student loans when I left. They only moved to Cramond after I finished my degree. I moved down to London then with Jack."

Maxwell couldn't help feeling a little narked even though he knew it was daft. While he'd been living on the streets turning tricks then clawing his way back into civilisation through a series of deadbeat jobs to support himself until he'd finally found his niche in becoming a flight attendant, Gibson had his own life all planned out, with a supportive family and loving parents.

What the hell do I have to show for my life? What do I have to offer someone like him who's going places? I couldn't even save Levi. He loved his drug dealer more than he loved me. How can this man ever want someone like me?

He moved away from interrupting Gibson as he worked, to sit cross-legged on the floor beside him, staring absently out of the window at the sky outside. His throat ached a bit as he thought about what he'd missed out on. He thought he'd grown content with his lot, but this new relationship had thrown things his way he believed he'd gotten over. He hunched forward, wrapping his arms around his knees as he tried to suppress the welling of emotion inside. He blamed the fact he'd been sick and his resistance was low for his present state of mind.

"Max, are you okay?" Gibson's voice was worried and Maxwell heard him get off the couch and come to kneel beside him. "Are you feeling sick again?"

Maxwell took a deep mental breath and turned to flash a smile at his concerned lover. "No, everything is fine. I wanted to let you get on in peace." He wanted to talk but didn't quite trust himself yet. Perhaps later might be better when he didn't feel as vulnerable.

Gibson's eyes narrowed. "Don't lie to me," he said softly and reached out and stroked Maxwell's cheek. "Your face says otherwise. Was it something I said?"

"Of course not. I enjoy hearing about you. I'm proud of you for achieving so much."

Gibson studied his face intently and Maxwell flushed. "What? I know I've been sick and not looking my best but stop staring at me like I've grown a mole or something."

Gibson didn't look convinced. "No mole. I thought maybe you'd remembered—" His mobile rung and he gave Maxwell one final scrutinising glance and went to answer it.

"Mum, this is a surprise. I wasn't expecting a call—"

Maxwell stood up and stretched, staring out the window into the street below. He was still out of sorts but tried to push those feelings away. He had a gorgeous boyfriend, a job he enjoyed even if it was getting on his tits a bit with the long hours, and a roof over his head. He needed to count his blessings rather than find new insecurities to torment himself with. In fact, he'd been planning on having a conversation with his company to see if there were any ground crew jobs going. The idea of not being up in the air all the time and spending more time with Gibson was appealing, especially after their last fight. He made a mental note to speak to Grant about it once he got back to work.

He turned to Gibson to tell him, only to find him huddled on the floor, back against the wall, his face white and eyes looking as if they'd seen the devil himself.

"Baby, what's wrong?" He hurried over to him. Gibson's hands clutched the phone on his lap and the quacking noise emanating from it sounded panicked. Maxwell squatted down beside him.

"Gibson, talk to me." His heart clenched in panic. Gibson simply stared at him and Maxwell recognised his expression; he was no stranger to shock. He prised the phone from his lover's cold and trembling hands and lifted it to his ear.

"Hello, this is Maxwell, Gibson's boyfriend. He's upset, what did you say to him?"

"Maxwell." The woman's voice sounded strained. "This is Doris Henry. Gibson's mum?"

"Oh, sorry." Maxwell stammered. "I didn't mean to be rude. I was worried about him."

Because he's fucking comatose on the floor and I can't bear the stricken look in his eyes.

"He's had some bad news," Doris said softly, a quaver in her voice. "His dad—Cliff—passed away this morning." Her voice broke but she carried on. "He had what we think was a stroke and it's all rather stressful here. I needed to tell him but I don't know how much he heard. He disappeared on me."

Maxwell stared down at Gibson's pale figure and his heart ached for his pain. "I'm so sorry," he said, feeling the words were inadequate but not knowing what else to say. "I'll take care of him, I promise. He's safe with me. Is there anything else I can do?"

"Look after my boy for me, please." The sniffles on the other end of the phone were breaking Maxwell's heart. "He and his dad were very close and he didn't get the chance to say goodbye. He's going to be devastated. Please take care of him. I'll call him later when I know more about what's happening. I know he'll want to come up here. Can you help him organise things?"

"Of course," Maxwell promised. He stared down at the blank face below him. "I'll put your number in my phone and send you a text then you'll have my number too. Mrs Henry?"

The soft sobs continued. "Thank you. I have to go, the doctor's here. Tell Gibson I'll call him later. Tell him I love him." The phone went dead. Maxwell put it down on the side table and sat down beside Gibson. He reached out and tried to pull him into an embrace. Gibson was still and unresponsive.

"Come here, love. God, I hate you're going through this." He finally got Gibson in his arms, face pressed against his chest. Gibson still hadn't said anything. "Your mum told me to tell you she loves you and she'll call you later." He got a half nod.

Gibson spoke. "I never gave him back his scarf."

Maxwell frowned. "What?"

Gibson sat up and got to his feet. He stared down at Maxwell, green eyes blank and a frozen look on his face. "He wanted his scarf back and I hadn't looked for it yet. He'll need it. I need to go home." He picked up his phone and went to the couch, where he started packing all his PC stuff into his laptop bag. Maxwell stood up and joined him. He knew the scarf wasn't needed now but he'd do anything to help Gibson get through this.

"I'll take you home. I'll get us a taxi. You're in no state for the train. We'll look for the scarf when we get you home."

Gibson nodded again jerkily as he stuffed clothing into a holdall. He stared around blankly, and spotted his laptop. He fingers moved across the keyboard, saving and shutting down his open applications, and then it too was relegated to the depths of his laptop bag.

Maxwell wished Gibson would cry, give way to whatever emotions were swirling in his head, but it didn't seem forthcoming.

Gibson stared around at the room. "Is the taxi coming?"

Maxwell fetched his phone, which sat on the dining table. "Shit, not yet. Bear with me. Let me get someone."

He made a quick call and arranged a taxi for ten minutes' time. Gibson was already at the door, holdall in one hand, laptop bag in the other. Maxwell reached out for the holdall and took it.

"Let me help you." He saw Gibson's jacket lying over the back of the couch and picked it up, along with his own brown bomber jacket.

Within a few minutes, they were downstairs, standing in the cool morning air as they waited for the taxi. Gibson had said nothing more. He stood still and silent, a look of what Maxwell could only call *nothing* on his face. Maxwell noticed his fingers tapping nervously at his side and reached over to hold those cold ones in his warm hands. Gibson's fingers stilled and a soft sigh escaped his lips.

"I'm here," Maxwell murmured. "Whatever you need."

When the taxi arrived, they got in and the short distance to Gibson's flat was done in silence. As they entered the flat, Jack sat at the dining room table and his face lit up when he saw them come in.

"Gibson, my man! I must say the dude behind you looks much better than when I last saw him. Maxwell, how are you feeling?"

Maxwell muttered a greeting as he dropped the holdall in the entrance and watched as Gibson struggled to say something.

Jack looked at him, confusion on his face. "Gib, what's wrong?"

Gibson's voice was flat as he put down his bag and moved past Jack towards his bedroom. "My dad's dead. I need to find his scarf." He disappeared into the hallway.

Jack's mouth gaped open and pity and sadness played across his face. "Jesus, what happened?"

Maxwell repeated what Mrs Henry had told him and Jack passed a hand over a stubbled chin. "This is gonna kill him." He realised what he'd said and went beet red. "I meant—"

Maxwell nodded as he gave a tired sigh. "I know what you mean. And it's true. He's been virtually catatonic since his mum called earlier. He's not dealing well at all." He cocked an eyebrow at a still shocked Jack. "Do you know what this thing is about the bloody scarf?"

Jack nodded. "Last time his mum called, Gib told me he needed to find it to take home for his dad. It's a football scarf his dad left here when he was here last time." He cast a worried glance towards the hallway. "I can't believe Cliff's gone, that's awful. He was like family to me."

"I'm sorry he told you the news like that." Maxwell placed a comforting hand on Jack's shoulder. "This must be a shock for you too."

"It is." Jack ran a hand through his unruly hair. "I suppose I'd better go try talk to him."

Maxwell snorted. "Good luck with that. I've been trying for the past hour. Maybe you'll have more success."

Jack shrugged. "Maybe." He turned and left the room.

An irrational flare of jealousy struck as Maxwell considered perhaps Gibson might turn to Jack for comfort instead of him. They had been friends since they were teenagers after all.

And isn't it all about Gibson feeling better and not my own stupid insecurities? Of course it is. Stop being such a twat.

And when Jack came back five minutes later muttering Gibson was a stubborn ass and needed his butt kicked, Maxwell couldn't help feel a little happier. He knew it was wrong. But he was only human.

"He's turning his damn cupboard inside out looking for that scarf and he doesn't want help," Jack growled but his eyes were a little red. "Least not from me. I think you should go mash some sense into him."

Maxwell sighed. "I'll try." He remembered he'd been supposed to text Gibson's mother. "Crap. I need to get his phone off him anyway so I can text his mum. Let me enter the den of doom and see whether I emerge alive."

They grinned awkwardly at each other. Jack looked sad and Maxwell flashed a sympathetic look at him as he left. When he got to Gibson's bedroom, he was stunned at the sight greeting his eyes. A closet full of clothes and underwear had vomited all over Gibson's normally neat room. The bed was filled with stacks of jeans, shirts, jackets and assorted boxers, briefs and some items Maxwell thought looked interesting but realised now wasn't the time to investigate further.

At first, he couldn't see Gibson. The wardrobe doors were open, the space inside empty like Mother Hubbard's cupboard. From somewhere beyond the piled clamour of fashion on the bed was the noise of quiet, heart-rending sobbing. The sound struck him to his core. Maxwell didn't know how many more times his man was going to cause his heart to ache and his eyes to prickle with tears.

Since he'd met Gibson, his inner hormonal teenage girl was on high alert.

He stepped over yet more jackets, coats and tee shirts, went around to the other side of the bed and found Gibson, face streaked with tears, sitting on the floor, a tattered old green and white scarf twisting in his hands. Red-rimmed, puffy eyes behind fogged-up spectacles stared up at him glassily as Maxwell sat down beside him.

"You found it," Maxwell whispered. His hand reached out and clasped fidgeting fingers in his. They were ice cold.

"It was right in the back of my cupboard," Gibson's voice was choked. "I'm not a football fan, so when my dad left it I chucked it in there. I always meant to get it out and give it back to him because he loved this scarf." Green eyes glistened with tears. "Now I'll never get to do that, Max."

His body shook as he broke down and Maxwell drew him closer, feeling warm tears soak his tee shirt. He murmured soothing noises and stroked Gibson's back, his hair, anywhere Maxwell could so Gibson could feel he was there. Maxwell cursed whatever deity controlled the motherfucking universe causing this pain and grief. He knew full well how it felt to have the people you loved the most die on you.

"Let it all out, baby," he muttered into Gibson's hair. "I'm not going anywhere."

He held the shaking, weeping man in his arms until he stilled, only the occasional hiccup and tremor wracking his body.

"I didn't get to see him before he died," Gibson finally sniffled. "I should have gone up there when I heard he was sick. Everyone thought it was the flu or something, no one thought anything was serious." His voice choked up.

Maxwell reached over and picked up an old tee shirt and dried Gibson's face gently, wiping away traces of tears and snot from his face. Gibson had seen Maxwell at his worst and he could do the same for him. He kissed Gibson's head. "Don't blame yourself for not being there. I know that's trite and easier said than done, but take it from somebody who knows. These things happen and there's nothing you can do about it."

Jack walked into the room, eyes searching, face worried. "Hey, sport," he said softly as he came over. "Are you okay?"

"I'm fine, thank you, but I'm not sure about my man." Maxwell quipped and was gratified when his reply caused a slight snort from Gibson. Jack sighed and sat down, Gibson now sandwiched between them.

"I'm sorry I blurted it out the way I did when I came in. It was cruel. I know you liked my dad too." Gibson looked up, shame on his face.

Jack reached over and chucked his chin. "Don't worry, you were upset, I get that. I'm sorry, Gib. Your dad was legend."

"Yes he was," Gibson replied, still clutching the scarf as he snuggled against Maxwell. The three men sat in silence for a while and then Maxwell grimaced.

"Gibson, can I have your phone please? I promised your mum I'd text her my number so I need hers."

Gibson shuffled and plucked his phone from his jeans pocket. He unlocked the screen and handed it over. Maxwell scrolled down and sent himself a message with Mrs Henry's number. In the lounge, his phone beeped. He wrested out of Gibson's grip and stood up.

"Be back in a min. Let me get it done before I forget."

When he got to his phone, he quickly sent Gibson's mother a text introducing himself then put his phone in his pocket in case she called. When he got back into the bedroom, Jack and Gibson were busy putting all the clothes back into cupboards and on shelves. The scarf was laid lovingly on Gibson's pillow.

Maxwell joined in and once the room was clear of abandoned fashion, he reached out and drew his lover into a hug. "Are you hungry? I can order your favourite pizza if you like. A Mighty Meaty. Like me." He smirked, hoping the old joke would make Gibson smile.

Jack groaned. "Enough, already. I don't need to hear your disgusting innuendos about how big your dicks are. I get enough of that from Gibson. Like what he said to me the other night when I threatened to rip his tongue out." He stopped abruptly as Maxwell grinned. Jack didn't know him well enough yet or he would never have made the remark.

Maxwell sniggered. "Wow, who knew your friends were so violent, Gibson?" He turned. "I happen to love your tongue. It has so many uses. Like when you wrap it around my—"

Jack made a disgusted noise like 'Gah' and fled the room.

"Ice cream cone. I was going to say ice cream cone, you dirty-minded dog." Maxwell said in an injured tone. He supposed the wide grin on his face didn't lend credence to his lie.

"God, Max, you are bad." Gibson's watery smile was a panacea to Maxwell's tender heart.

"Yep, I have that badge already. And what did you say to him the other night anyway?"

Gibson grinned fleetingly. "I asked him how I was going to rim guys without my tongue."

"Oh, God," Maxwell's cick gave a sly, happy nod at the thought. It was one of his favourite things to have done to him so a Gibson without his tongue was inconceivable.

Crap. I need to stop thinking about sex. My boyfriend has lost his father, you animal.

"Jack seems like a cool guy. I like him."

Gibson nodded. "He's a peach. He and Beth are the best. She's funny and keeps him in line I love her to bits."

How about me? Do you maybe love me a little? God, I'm such a needy bastard.

"Do you need to call your mum back now you're feeling a little better or do you want to wait until she calls you?"

Gibson's face shadowed. "I need to get home to help Mum and Ricky with all the arrangements." His face set stubbornly. "I'm not letting them do everything on their own. I'll take a look at flights and get up there soon as I can."

Maxwell shook his head. "Leave it. I'll do it for you. I used to work in travel. I'll get you sorted. Maybe I can even reschedule some of my flights and go with you earlier." He'd call Grant to see what he could do to get whatever shifts he had changed. They'd originally only been due to fly out to Chloe's birthday next week. Maxwell wished with all his heart fate had given Gibson those extra days to at least see his dad one last time.

Gibson flashed him a grateful smile. "Thanks, I appreciate that. My head's all messed up. I want to sleep for a bit. I'm actually not hungry much after all." He looked longingly at his bed.

"Get in there and wallow for a bit. I'll go sort stuff out and come check on you in a little while. We'll get that pizza later then."

Gibson needed no urging and soon he was naked, his body sliding under his duvet. He clutched the scarf in his hands. His face was still pale, his eyes swollen. Maxwell wanted to undress and lie beside him, cuddle him until all the hurt went away. But he had work to do getting Gibson to what remained of his family.

Chapter 11

Gibson stared out of the plane window, seeing little and not in the mood to appreciate the beauty of the clouds and sea below. His brain hadn't functioned properly since he'd learnt of his father's death. Well, that, plus Max's fevered mutterings when he'd been sick. Gibson was still processing that unguarded conversation about the things he'd done on the streets and the words 'I think I love you.' He had a heavy feeling in the pit of his stomach he knew what Max might tell him what he'd done to survive when he was homeless.

And Gibson wouldn't judge him if it was what he thought it was.

But the worry had taken a backseat in the face of his dad's death; he could only manage one momentous event at a time. When he was stronger, he'd ask Max about 'those things' and tell him they didn't matter.

Beside him Max shifted, his longer legs trying to find comfort in the crowded aeroplane. "I'm more used to being out there than in here," he moaned as he shuffled his backside on the seat and waved a hand at the cabin crew. One of them rolled her eyes and Gibson snorted softly in agreement. The crew had been attentive to them and were a pleasant bunch. One of them had even commiserated with Gibson on landing the 'Maxwell fish,' but she'd said it with a gleam in her eye and a fond smile. It appeared everyone loved Max.

Gibson smiled faintly. "Stop complaining. We're nearly there." He idly fingered the green and white scarf around his neck. He checked his laptop bag was still under his seat and gave a sigh of relief. He didn't know whether he'd get in any game development while he was away but he didn't travel anywhere without his laptop.

Max had pulled in every favour he could to get them on the earliest flight to Edinburgh a day later. Gibson still didn't know how he'd managed it.

When he'd asked, Max had jokingly told him he'd threatened to release some rather risqué pictures of his boss, Grant, to his wife that Max had taken at a rather drunken stopover one night in Naples. Gibson still wasn't sure if Max had been serious. Sometimes he couldn't tell.

There was one thing worrying him. He'd overheard Max agreeing to take unpaid time off to accompany him back to his family. Max could ill afford that.

"Tell me again you didn't have to sell your soul to come with me this week?" He turned to look at Max who stopped fidgeting and stared back. "I mean, you'd been sick, then this—did you have the leave due?"

Max frowned. "I told you. It's fine. We get to use my airline discount to save some money. Driving us up wasn't an option because my decrepit Punto wouldn't have made it. And hiring one would have cost a small fortune. Stop worrying. It'll be extra for the taxi fare to your house."

Gibson sighed. "Sorry. I'm on edge I guess." He turned to stare out the window again. A warm hand reached out and caressed his cheek. He looked back into his lover's warm brown eyes.

"Gibson, I know the funeral is only in a couple of weeks but I think I'm more useful to you now as support. I'm sorry I can't be there with you but I'll never get the time off." Max's face crinkled in a look of guilt.

Gibson leaned over and kissed Max's lips, not caring who saw it. "I appreciate it, honest. Seeing my mum and brother is going to kill me, and *not* seeing my dad." He tried to get past the lump in his throat as tears threatened. "I'll be able to face it better if you're there with me this time around."

The intercom crackled and the captain announced they were preparing to land. As Gibson pushed his tray up and handed over the remnants of the food he hadn't yet eaten—he had no appetite—he was thankful for Max's reassuring presence beside him. In a short time, the man had become someone special, someone beloved. It scared the crap out of Gibson.

First things first. Dealing with his father's death was going to be tough enough.

*****

When he stepped up to the front door of the small, honeysuckle-festooned cottage in a lane set back among fields and cows, the impending family reunion was everything Gibson had both dreaded and looked forward to.

His mother's pale, grief-stricken face set with a brave smile and his brother Richard's bear hug as he held Gibson tightly and whispered he was glad to see him all conspired to make Gibson a gibbering wreck.

The mongrel greeting Gibson with such excitement had him in tears as he knelt down and buried his face in the thick fur. When he stood up, his face surely a mess, the three family members stood, in a group hug, crying, comforting each other and murmuring words of love and support. It was only when his mother finally released him and he could draw a breath that he realised Max was still standing awkwardly on the doorstep with a dog sniffing at his crotch.

Gibson wiped his eyes and nose on the sleeve of his tee shirt and motioned to a Max who looked ready to turn and run like a hound. He guessed Max wasn't used to loud, emotional displays of affection or family antics.

"Haggis, leave Max alone. Mum, Ricky, this is my boyfriend, Max Lewis. He'll be staying a few days with me."

If Gibson hadn't been so emotional he might have laughed at the panicked expression on his lover's face was he was enfolded into Doris Henry's big arms, his face pressed against a soft bosom.

"Max, lovely to meet you, child, even under the circumstances. I've heard nothing about you so I look forward to getting to know you." Max looked spooked, his eyes widening. He cast a panicked glance at Gibson who took pity on him.

"God, Mum, please let him go, before you kill him with kindness from those boobs of yours."

His mother tut-tutted but released the man currently looking as if he was being consumed with motherly affection. Doris's eyes widened when she finally noticed what Gibson wore around his neck. She reached out and touched the scarf with reverence.

"You found it." she breathed. "I don't believe it..." She burst into tears again as Gibson took the scarf off and wrapped it around her neck as once again he and his brother comforted their mother.

It was Ricky's turn to say hello. He held a hand out to Max and nodded, but there was speculation in his blue eyes. The sort that said, 'You hurt my little brother and I'll pluck out your eyes and feed them to you.'

If Gibson hadn't been feeling so raw he might have found it funny. Instead he watched as Max shook hands and murmured pleasantries and consolations. They were all ushered through to a big, warm farmhouse kitchen filled with various plates containing cakes, foil-wrapped secrets and various pastries dotting brightly coloured platters.

Doris gave a shrug. "The neighbours have been around, taking care of us. They're good souls but the doorbell hasn't stopped ringing."

His mother sounded exhausted and Gibson leaned in and gave her another hug. "It's going to be okay," he whispered as his throat clogged up. "We'll all get through this. Dad wouldn't want us falling apart."

His mum nodded. "I know, Gibson. I miss him so much."

"Me too," Gibson managed. She didn't need to know how much he'd fallen apart since her phone call or how Max had pulled him up from his doldrums more than once. "Maybe when we're sitting down I can hear the rest of the story and what happened. I know I've been putting it off but I want to know the whole story."

Doris nodded and moved away to pick up the kettle and fill it up. "I'll make us some tea then we can have a sit down. Go get your stuff out the car, love, and take it up to your room. We can have tea in the drawing room."

An hour later, curled up on the couch with Haggis and Max on either side of him, Gibson knew everything more he needed to know about his father's death. It was simple. It hadn't been a stroke. Cliff Henry had been over working, unwell from a bout of flu, which had debilitated him, and then he suffered a pulmonary embolism. Tragically, nothing could have been done and he was dead by the time the ambulance got him to the hospital.

Gibson noticed Max's reaction when his mother confirmed it had been an embolism. He'd drawn in a breath, a shadow of pain crossing his face.

That means something to him.

Gibson reached out and touched Max's hand. Sienna coloured eyes regarded him with darkness in their depths.

"Babe, are you okay?" Gibson asked in concern.

Max nodded jerkily. "Yeah. It's..." He cleared his throat. "The same thing happened to my mother. An embolism."

"Oh I'm sorry to hear that, Max," Doris Henry said softly. "This must bring back bad memories for you then."

Max shook his head. "She died in childbirth. With me. I never knew her." He fidgeted with his hands. Gibson reached out and laid a comforting hand on Max's arm. Even though Gibson knew this already, his heart still ached for what Max must be going through reliving the circumstances of his birth.

Doris leaned over and clasped Max's hand in sympathy. "Do you have other family?"

Gibson saw the wariness creeping into Max's face. He wanted to ask his mother not to go down that road in case it led to well-meaning questions about his past. Max would no doubt be mortified if Gibson's family found about his street past.

"No. They're dead too. I have no family." Max rolled a shoulder as if it was hurting. "It's only me." The finality in his tone was a warning to anyone not to pursue the topic.

"And me," Gibson said, rubbing his thumb over Max's hand. "Remember? Blond, sexy fabulous cute guy you picked up on a plane?"

Richard snorted and Doris laughed. "That's how you met? Sounds like a great story."

Both Max and Gibson flushed. That wasn't a story they were sharing anytime soon. Gibson had a feeling that to his mother and brother, a blowjob and jack-off in a bathroom stall was not the stuff of true romance.

"But he *is* all of those things," Max murmured, looking at Gibson with an expression that made him want to run up to his room with Max right now and have his way with him.

Gibson's mother smiled. "Oh my," she said softly. "I think you made a good choice here, son. I like him."

Gibson heaved a sigh of relief later that night when he and Max were finally alone in his room. It wasn't late, only eight o'clock, but he'd seen his mother flagging, and Richard had wanted to get back to his own family a few miles down the road. They'd all been overwhelmed and decided an early night was the best idea. Tomorrow they'd go over the final funeral and cremation arrangements, the songs being sung and the eulogies and then hopefully things would be in place to say a final goodbye.

Gibson snickered when he opened his bedside drawer and saw the items in there. "Mum's been busy." He held up a string of about twelve condoms, large and medium sizes, and snorted again.

"You're only here three nights. What does she think we're going to do—fuck like bunnies?" He held up the mid-size bottle of lube. "Bubble-gum flavoured. I've not tasted it before." His face shadowed. "I'm not sure I'm up for much, though."

Max leaned over and hugged him. "Being here by your side is enough for me. I want you to try to get some sleep tonight. You haven't been lately."

Gibson watched in fascination as Max laid out his clothes in piles. Underwear. Tee shirts. Jeans and sweatpants. Multi-coloured columns of varying sizes and textures making short stacks leaning like the Tower of Pisa.

"You know that's a chest of drawers, right?" he remarked. "You can actually put the stuff *inside* the drawers."

Max nodded. "I know. I like it this way." He continued unpacking, one final short pile containing two thin pullovers. Warmth flooded Gibson as he observed his quirky man. He didn't understand the need inside Max to have his things close to hand and on display, but he appreciated he needed to. Gibson stepped up and wrapped his arms around Max's waist.

"Have I told you how much I'm thankful you're here with me?" he whispered against Max's tee shirt. Gibson pressed his ear to Max's back, listening to the faint heartbeat.

Max's arms reached backwards, encircling him as he leaned back into Gibson. "You have, but I like hearing it," was the quiet reply.

"You ground me," Gibson whispered as he closed his eyes to the steady throb of the heart beneath his ear. "Make me strong so I believe I can get through this. You help me forget for a while."

And wasn't that the truth. He'd gone from Gibson the Unbeliever to Gibson the Fallen with this man. The sense of belonging to someone, along with the knowledge he too possessed something he wanted and needed, was a revelation.

Max twisted around to face him. His eyes shone; whether it was moisture or the soft light in the room reflecting off his dark pupils, Gibson wasn't sure. He didn't care because Max was kissing him, sweet, gentle kisses with a warm wet tongue and lips tasting of tea and shortcake biscuits.

As they stood there, pressed against each other, mouths exploring and breaths feeding each other's passion, Gibson wondered fleetingly if Max would ever be one hundred percent conscious and tell him again he loved him. He wanted to be sure; he didn't want those words to have been fuelled only by fever and paracetamol.

Later, lying cuddled up beside Max after a satisfying session of nothing more than stroking each other to release, both of them breathless between moaning gasps uttered in the darkness of his bedroom, Gibson wondered if he'd ever say the words back if they were said to him.

*****

The next morning when Gibson and Max came downstairs at eight-thirty, there was a full cooked breakfast on the table. His mother looked tired and strained.

Gibson scolded her. "Mum, you didn't have to get up early to make breakfast. Max and I would have had cereal or something."

He poured coffee for him and tea for Maxwell as his boyfriend stood uncertainly at Gibson's side

Doris flapped a dishtowel in their direction. "I couldn't sleep, so I got up to cook. It gave me something useful to do." She scurried around the kitchen putting bacon, fried tomato and eggs together with slices of fried bread onto white plates. "Sit, Maxwell. You're a guest in my house. The least I can do is feed you boys."

Breakfast was a sombre affair. Haggis scrounged scraps, which Gibson fed him guiltily off his plate, hoping his mother didn't see, and Max ate his toast, not saying much. It was clear he was uncomfortable with the whole family environment. Gibson's ex-fuck buddy Jamie knocked on the door as they were drying up dishes, and rushed in to embrace Gibson with a wet, smacking kiss with a hint of tongue then murmured with a soft Scottish lilt, "God, I'm so sorry about your dad." Max didn't look charmed. His eyes smouldered, his lips curled and the look of venom he threw Jamie's way would have killed an entire army in their tracks.

Gibson hadn't been prepared for the welcome and he hastily extricated himself from the body pressed against his, determinedly removed the groping hands on his arse and glared at Jamie.

"Shit, Jamie, stop mauling me in front of my boyfriend."

Jamie's not-so-innocent blue eyes under his droopy fringe of brown hair widened as he looked comically at Gibson then at the snarling Max. Gibson shivered in delight seeing possessiveness in Max's eyes. He knew he shouldn't feel this way but it turned him on.

"Oh, I'm sorry, Gibson. I didn't know."

"Yes you did," Doris Henry said. "I told you about him, Jamie. You're taking a chance." She smiled faintly as she turned to the sink and plunged her hands into the soapy bubbles.

"Well, I forgot." Jamie's lips pursed into a moue of displeasure as he stared appraisingly at Max. "This is the new guy? Huh." He didn't sound impressed.

Gibson suddenly wanted to snort in laughter at the look crossing Max's face, a look of indignation and dislike. Gibson needed to head this off at the pass. He crossed to Max and rose on his toes, reaching up to place a soft kiss on Max's tight lips.

"Max, this is Jamie. He's an—" He struggled for the right word. Ex didn't seem the right word for mutual blowjobs and jerk-offs. Fuck buddy would be frowned upon by his mother, although technically it was the right term.

"Friend," he said lamely. "Jamie, this is Max. My *boyfriend*." He made sure to enunciate the words. Max's face relaxed a little but he still looked at Jamie as if he was dog dirt on his shoe. Gibson held tightly to Max's hand.

"Whatever." Jamie waved a dismissive hand in Max's direction. "Gibson, I'm so sorry about your dad, my lovely. Is there anything I can do?"

Gibson shook his head, his throat clenching at the concern in Jamie's voice. "No, but thank you. Not unless you can bring him back."

The younger man's round face softened. "I wish I could, baby. I wish I could." Gibson winced as Max's hand tightened around his at the endearment.

Jamie looked at Doris. "Mrs H, you look tired. Can I do the washing up for you? You take a seat and I'll finish up while these guys dry up." He gently pushed her out of the way and took over. Doris rolled her eyes at Gibson and moved away to sit at the kitchen table. Gibson wondered how much of a visitor Jamie had been to his home while he'd been gone. He and his mother appeared comfortable with each other. The same couldn't be said about Max.

He finished drying up in silence then muttered something about having a phone call to make and disappeared out into the garden.

Gibson glared at Jamie. "You've upset him," he accused. His heart was already heavy with grief and the last thing he wanted was his rock rolling away downhill. "You shouldn't have kissed me. We're not an item anymore, remember?"

Jamie stared at him wide eyed. "I'm sorry, Gibson. I suppose I got carried away. He seems a little…standoffish. Are you sure he's right for you?"

Gibson scowled at him fiercely. "He's perfect for me." And how true were those words. Gibson had never expected to say them, especially not so soon after starting a relationship. "He's not used to family; he's been on his own fending for himself since he was fourteen years old and he's learnt to hide himself away from people."

Gibson's mother drew in a horrified breath. "Alone since he was fourteen? What happened?"

He had no desire to tell anything of what he knew of Mooch's dark tale. That was Max's story to tell should he ever want to, and even Gibson was waiting for it. "He lost his whole family and went to foster care. But he's amazing, Mum. He's warm, he's funny and he looks after me. I lo—like him. And he likes me."

He loves me in fact. Gibson held the thought close to him.

Jamie looked shame faced. "Okay, well, I'm sorry. I miss you. But I guess I need to get over it."

Gibson nodded. "He's special, Jamie. I need to go see how he's doing. Mum, you okay?"

Doris waved a hand. "Go find your fella, Gibson. We'll be fine." She grinned faintly. "Jamie, have I told you about that young man at the youth centre, who thinks you're cute? His name is Dennis…"

As his mother did her gay matchmaking, Gibson left Jamie expressing horror at the thought of dating a man called Dennis and hurried off to find Max. He found him leaning on the old white picket fence, staring out across the grey expanse of the sea, as the wind blew his hair across his face and turned his cheeks ruddy. Gibson thought he'd never seen a more heart-stopping sight.

"You okay?" Gibson asked softly. "I'm sorry about Jamie. He can get a bit much."

Max shrugged. "Not your fault. This is your home, your family and your past. I'm a guest."

A pang snapped through Gibson's chest like a rubber band being launched inside him. "Max, you're my boyfriend. My family is yours. What's wrong?"

Max cleared his throat. "I guess I'm not used to family things. It's been such a long time I don't know how to act. Like offering to do the dishes for your mum. Jamie didn't even hesitate about it, but it didn't even occur to me…"

Gibson reached up and framed Max's face in his hands. "Stop it. No one expects anything of you. Being here for me is enough." He pulled him closer, feeling Max's body respond to his closeness as they stood together in the garden trading tender, gentle kisses.

Max sighed into his mouth, whispers of tea-scented breath and toothpaste. Part of Gibson wanted to hear Max say those words again, those ones he'd uttered in the dim, medicinal depths of his bedroom. The other part of him still worried about what might happen if he did.

They drew apart, mouths swollen, eyes darkened with the knowledge that perhaps later they'd be able to fulfil their need for each other again in the privacy of Gibson's room.

"Are you doing okay?" Max reached and brushed a strand of hair from Gibson's face. "This is about you, not me. I want to try and make you feel better, not the other way around."

Gibson nodded at the reminder of why he was home. "I feel pretty raw inside, but I need to be strong for my mum. She might look strong but she's fragile, I can tell. She and my dad were close. They were married thirty years, and now he's gone."

Max drew him closer, a comforting, strong presence he fell into, closing his eyes as he breathed in Max's scent. They stood for a while, simply feeding each other with spoonfuls of solidarity and familiarity.

"I'm sorry I can't talk about my past much," Max murmured sadly. "It's not something I want to share. It's sordid."

Gibson snuggled in. "I don't know much about it either," he said gently. "I know you were on the streets with someone called Levi who you obviously loved, and he died. I know how you ended up there and I've picked up things here and there. That's about it."

Max drew a deep breath. "I don't want to tell you about the stuff I did then," he muttered. "I don't want to see disgust in your eyes."

Gibson hugged him. Max had said as much when he'd been fevered and sick. "I could never be that man. I wouldn't judge you. I *want* to hear it. Max, baby, that's what boyfriends do. They listen."

There was silence. When Max spoke again his voice was pained. "Levi and I were lovers. He showed me the ropes. We ran away together because he told me it would be better. And for a while it was. Then he got hooked on drugs, and it spiralled down from there. Sometimes he was so out of it, I had to find the money to help us survive." Max shuddered. "I found I could get easy money for food and shelter being a rent boy on the streets."

Gibson moved and looked up into shadowed eyes. "I suspected as much," he said, lifting a hand to touch Max's cheek. "And listen when I tell you I don't care. You did what you needed to do. To keep you and Levi alive."

Max laughed harshly. "I was lucky I didn't pick up any diseases, but I always insisted on condoms. I guess it paid off." His eyes grew distant. "I sat down next to Levi for over an hour before I realised he was dead." His voice choked. "I even kicked him to try wake him up for fuck's sakes. The cops arrived and carted us both off, to a shelter. I was dehydrated, starving, malnourished and full of lice. At the shelter they sorted me out." His tone grew soft. "There was this policeman, the one who found us. He was so damn kind. He had a sixteen-year-old kid at home so he could empathise, I guess. I fell apart, and he was there for me. It kills that I never knew his name, to say thank you afterwards. I tried to track him down but couldn't find him." He sighed heavily. "I buried Levi and then turned my life around."

Gibson traced the lone tear trickling down Max's cheek. "I don't care what you did back then. I think you did good, babe. I mean look at you now." His own eyes stung. "I'm so glad you made it through. I can't imagine not having you in this world."

They stood together in a fierce embrace, staring out at the windswept sea. Later in the night when Max slid inside him with a soft sigh and a kiss, offering Gibson everything he needed and wanted, Gibson wondered how he'd ever existed without this man.

Chapter 12

The flight home a few days later was lonely, unwelcomed and too soon. Maxwell was glad he'd managed to organise that he worked on the return flight and it was hectically busy. It kept his mind off seeing Gibson's slim figure and pale face standing at the gate as he'd waved goodbye to the taxi taking Maxwell to the airport. Laying himself raw and spilling his guts had unsettled Maxwell, but it had been a long time coming, and it had been time for Gibson to know more.

His feelings about Jamie being there instead of him were enough to make him a little bitter. He trusted Gibson but not Jamie. The situation rankled and burned in his gut. The only shining light was Jack and Beth were coming up to attend the funeral. Maxwell was confident they'd be there for Gibson when he couldn't be.

Home. When he walked in around eleven pm, his flat appeared empty. Gibson's red and white jersey lay on the couch, no doubt left there after a frantic session making out when they'd divested themselves of clothes, eager to be with each other. A pair of Gibson's worn trainers lay under the coffee table, the ones he used to go walking in when they decided to go down to the river and watch the container ships pass by. They bought fish and chips while sitting and imagining what the cargo was and where the ships were headed.

Everywhere Maxwell turned there was a reminder of Gibson. Crumpled up pieces of paper in the waste bin was evidence of perceived failed renderings of Gibson's creativity, at least according to him. Maxwell though they were incredible. His lover had an artistic talent for drawing that blew Maxwell's mind.

Books were stacked neatly on the sideboard, instead of being sprawled across the room. His possessions were tidied up and packed away and Maxwell simply hadn't bothered to take them out again to their original position. The need to display the things he owned wasn't as important to him anymore. He had something more valuable now than stuff.

He unpacked, had a shower, changed into comfortable clothes and made himself noodles. He pulled out his bed, switched on the television and watched Nigella creating some fabulous dish but he didn't quite take it all in. His mind was still in Scotland with a man dealing with his father's death and trying to be strong for his family.

He picked up his phone and sent Gibson a text.

Hey baby. Got home safely. How you doing? xxoo

He watched Nigella folding some concoction of meats into pastry as he waited impatiently for a reply. It came ten minutes later.

Glad you're safe. Miss you already tho. I'm doing okay. xx

Wish I was there. I feel crap coming home without you. House is empty. No sexy Gibson driving me crazy.

Haha. Giving you a rest from my crazy. There was an emoticon of a smiley face rolling his eyes.

I like your crazy. How's your mum? Maxwell wanted to ask about whether Jamie was still hanging around but he didn't want to seem needy or insecure—even though he knew he was.

Holding up. She's tough. Her friends are rallying around. My uncle is here. He flew in from Wales earlier today. We're all good.

Maxwell experienced the familiar pang of longing to be there with a family that rallied around in tough times. His phone pinged again.

Got a message from Cruz. He's still in Rio, not coming back still for a while. I think they're planning on moving over there.

Maxwell knew Gibson missed his friend. He still hadn't met the man properly other than at the club.

The next text lifted his spirits.

Jamie left today too. He's gone back home, he's going on holiday tomorrow with his brother to Ibiza.

Maxwell sighed with relief. He could afford to be magnanimous now.

Oh I wasn't worried about him. Ibiza sounds cool. Maybe one day we'll get there together? Partying, drinking cocktails, sex on the beach?

Firstly - liar with a capital L Secondly are you talking about the drink or something else?

Maxwell scowled. He'd been rumbled. He chose to ignore the liar remark.

Both of them. He found a gif of someone—one of the Three Stooges, he thought—raising bushy eyebrows over and over again in a suggestive fashion and sent it.

Lol, I thought so. You are such a bad boy.

"You have no idea," Maxwell murmured with a satisfied smile. He lay back on the couch and propped a cushion under his head as he got comfortable. Maybe a little sexting would take Gibson's mind off things for a little while.

Are you in bed?

Yeah...?

What are you wearing? Maxwell sniggered.

I wish it was you. Instead I'd have to say the little black thong you like.

Maxwell groaned. He did love Gibson's little thong, which showed his pert arse to perfection but he doubted he was wearing it to bed. The little bastard was messing with him.

Oh? All I'm wearing is my hand on my cock.

It was no lie. Maxwell was already stroking himself as he arranged his phone on the pillow next to him, waiting for the next text. His dick was already hard and thinking of Gibson in the thong was making it harder.

There was a delay before his boyfriend replied.

Do you wish it was my hand on your cock instead? Like this?

Maxwell moaned as he released his cock to read the full text. It had been accompanied with a picture of a cherished item he recognised, a familiar hand wrapped around it teasingly.

He hastily sent a quick text back with hands sticky with his own pre-come. He'd have to clean his screen later.

God, you are sexy and such a bitch tease. Now I have to jerk off, so I'll be a while.

Take your time. I'm busy this side too, thinking of you being inside me. Feeling you fill me with your gorgeous cock.

Maxwell closed his eyes and his back arched as he thrust upwards into his hand, thinking of Gibson doing the same thing miles away. He smelt Gibson on the pillows still, saw his green eyes in his memory, experienced the warmth of his skin against his as he trembled and bucked beneath him, needy and wanton, his muscles clenching around Maxwell's cock as he orgasmed.

Maxwell gave a cry of release as his own fluids spilled over his hands onto the cover, leaving him gasping and spent. For a few minutes he lay there, drowsy and replete. His phone beeped again.

God. I wish you were here. I came like a freight train thinking of you.

Maxwell wiped his hands on his ever-available wet wipes and picked up his phone.

Me too. Want you here so badly to fall asleep beside. Miss you so much already.

He wanted so badly to write the words he wanted to say but it wasn't fair to do that to Gibson right now. He had enough going on in his life without an 'I love you' being sprung on him when he was at his most vulnerable.

His phone beeped again.

Knackered now. Need to sleep. Me and mum going to the funeral home tomorrow to finalise arrangements. I'll call you tomorrow night xx

K. Sleep tight lover. Speak tomorrow. Can't wait. ♥

Maxwell put down his phone and sighed ruefully as he regarded the sticky mess across his belly and duvet. Time to clean up then hit the sack and dream about tender green eyes staring into his.

*****

A week later, Maxwell went into work—he'd been putting in as many hours as he could while Gibson was away—but Maxwell wasn't flying this time. He had an interview with the manager of the ground crew at London City. He was a little nervous.

Benjamin Sibonga had a body built like a rugby forward and was reputed to be a hardnosed, tough, but fair man. He was well respected by both his crew and the airport personnel alike, and his cheery Ugandan visage was always apparent as he wandered the airport like a man on a mission to ensure everything was running well. Maxwell left the interview nearly two hours later, drained, sweating and feeling as if he was one of the unfortunates at the bottom of the scrum in Benjamin's rugby team. The *interrogation*, as Maxwell grumpily called it, had been gruelling and tiring. The walk around the airport in his guided tour had been a fast-paced, no-holds-barred look at what went on down on the ground.

Maxwell knew working as ground crew would be vastly different to being in the air— helping to guide the aircraft into the gate, loading and unloading luggage from the plane, preparing the paperwork and fuel requirements for the pilot, and embarking and disembarking passengers onto the aircraft. It was all hectic, physical work. But it was more stable and less hours than flying, and he got to go home each day with no lengthy stay-overs or days away from home. Despite his love of being in the air, Maxwell loved the idea of coming home to Gibson, being able to spend more time with him, perhaps even plan a trip to Ibiza or somewhere else.

He had to wait a few days for the rest of the interviews to be concluded then Benjamin had promised to call him to let him know one way or another. Gibson would be home in a week's time and Maxwell hoped to be able to give him some good news. At least, he hoped Gibson would see it as good news.

Before he'd left for Scotland, worried he'd made the wrong call about changing jobs, Maxwell had called Oliver about it. His friend had been supportive.

"Max, you care about this guy. Being together a bit more can only be good for your relationship. Besides, the money's better too, isn't it?"

Maxwell sighed as he held his mobile phone to his ear with one hand. "Yeah, a little better. But what if he doesn't want to see me more? I mean, Gibson is used to so much more. He's actually *going* places, and here I am working at an airport and eking out a living."

I was a homeless rent boy with a deceased drug addict for a partner. Could he accept that?

"Stop it." Oliver's voice was fierce. "You had a tough time and you dragged yourself up. You've never told me exactly what happened when you were a kid and I don't need to know. The man I know now is not a nobody, Max. He's a tough, strong man who deserves more. Don't for fuck's sake be like me and try to push away the best thing that ever happened to you. It'll make you miserable. Gibson makes you happy. Stick with him."

"I know," Maxwell had whispered. "But when I finally tell him all the things I did back then, to keep alive, what if he hates me for it? What if I disgust him, Ollie?" It was the closest he'd ever come to telling anyone else what he'd been all that time ago. He closed his eyes as he'd waited for Oliver's reply.

When it came his friend's voice was heavy with compassion. "Baby, whatever you did to survive when you were a kid, he'll understand. From what I've seen, Gibson is very into you. I doubt he'll be put off by your sordid stories of days past. Trust me."

Maxwell was humbled by Oliver's understanding. "I hope so." He took a deep breath. "I love him, Oliver. I never thought I'd say that to anyone." *Not since Levi.*

Oliver's voice had a smile in it when he next spoke. "I'd never have guessed from the goo-goo eyes you made at him when we had dinner together. Leslie said he was already planning which wedding suit to wear to the Big Day. A Debussy of course."

Maxwell scowled. "Bite me, buster. I do so not make goo-goo eyes at people."

His friend laughed loudly. "You keep telling yourself that. I know what I saw."

Maxwell smiled as he rung off as he remembered the dinner conversation. Oliver had been right.

Maxwell took another sip of his tea then his eyes were drawn to a news story on the television about drugs. He turned up the volume.

"The young woman who was arrested in Indonesia a month ago on charges of drug trafficking is now facing the death penalty. She was allegedly found with over ten pounds of heroin in her possession when she was searched at the airport. Her parents have started a campaign to get her freed but at this stage it is unlikely that will happen."

He turned down the volume as he muttered angrily. "People go into countries known for having the death penalty for drugs, taking their stuff in and then when they get caught they expect to be treated differently? Don't do that kind of thing in the first place, lady. Can't do the time, don't do the crime."

When Levi had died, the post mortem that had been done had discovered he'd been subjected to some *very bad shit*. Shit that had been cut with every nasty thing imaginable and caused Levi's heart to stop, his throat to swell up and vomit to gush from his mouth. It was why Maxwell hated the smell and look of puke even now.

Once he'd been strong enough, he'd gone back on the streets, trying to find the dealer who sold the bad shit to Levi—to no avail. It was probably best because Maxwell didn't know what he would have done had he found the bastard. Back then his values had been skewed, his psyche fucked up and his ethics dubious. Beating some low-life dealer to death in a back alley as retribution for the death of the man he'd loved might not have been a stretch.

"And that is the one thing I *never* want to tell Gibson," he murmured as he stuck a lasagne ready meal in the microwave. "It's too much. I don't want him to feel he has to sleep with one eye open in case the psycho side of me comes calling."

When his phone rang four days later with a familiar number, Maxwell closed his eyes and hoped it was good news.

"Maxwell? It's Benjamin here. How are you?"

He crossed his fingers. "Fine, thank you. It's good to hear from you."

Benjamin gave a great belly laugh. "Of course it is. Especially when you hear my news. You are on the team, my friend. Your personal references checked out, and Grant says he'll be unhappy to lose you but I couldn't get a better employee."

Maxwell had been ready to do his personal Gilda Gray shimmy when he'd heard 'you are on the team' but hearing his future boss say his last boss thought he was worth it made him want to add a little break dancing into his moves. "Oh that's awesome news, thank you so much. You won't be sorry."

"I'd better not be," Benjamin growled. "Everyone wants to work on my team because we are the best and look after each other. I turned down a lot of applications to give you this job, so I will expect you to work hard and be part of the family."

Maxwell grinned. "Not a problem. I think I can do that. I'm truly pleased." And he was. He knew he'd miss flying but being with Gibson more than made up for it. As long as Gibson thought so too.

After he put the phone down and did his little dance around the room, he fell onto the couch in a contemplative mood. He started his new job in a month's time, with a generous increase in salary and benefits. He might even be able to start that savings account he'd always wanted if he was clever; then perhaps next year he and Gibson could go on holiday somewhere.

"Beach, sea, blue skies, cocktails, sex and more sex," he sighed as he dreamed about the future. "Gibson in a speedo, a white one, all wet..." That thought was leading to sensations he'd have to deal with, but right now his stomach was rumbling and he needed to eat. Warding off a hard-on at the thought of his beautiful man in wet beachwear, Maxwell took himself off to the Turkish diner down the road for a celebratory meal. After a plate of alinazik, a bellyful of sweet syrupy baklava and more than a few of small glasses of raki,

Maxwell was merry and satiated. He staggered back to his flat inebriated and happy, where he continued to think of Gibson in his wet Speedos. He fell asleep contented, spent and eager for Gibson to come home so he could share the news and have the real thing in his bed.

*****

Coming home a few days after the funeral was bittersweet. One part of Gibson wanted to stay with his mother and brother as the closest links he had to his dad; the other half was eager to see Max again, to crawl into bed beside him and be held as if he was precious. Gibson always knew he could count on Max to make him feel that way. He'd done a lot of thinking while standing watching his father's coffin enter the flaming furnace consigning him to ashes.

He'd resigned himself to the fact Max was more than a passing phase. The past two weeks, not seeing him and needing him, had brought that home. Seeing the vulnerability when Max told him about his past had near broken Gibson's heart.

After Gibson got home that evening, he unpacked his bags and put his laptop away, thankful he'd managed to get a little work done while he'd been gone. He showered then changed into some of his sexiest clothing—his favourite Andrew Christian thong, tight black jeans making his arse perky and a soft, loose-fitting silk shirt that clung to his body—and made his way to Max's flat.

Max wasn't there; his flight was apparently on its way back from Venice and would be landing within the next hour. Gibson let himself into the flat with the ravish key and settled down to wait for Max's return.

His phone rang and he answered it. "Jack, hi. Sorry, you weren't home when I got in and I've come straight out to see Max."

Jack's voice always lifted Gibson's spirits. "No worries, munchkin. I was over at Beth's, her dog's been ill and he needed to go the vet again. I helped her get him there and it took bloody ages." His voice softened. "You okay? It was a grand funeral, Gibson. You gave your dad a real send off. Beth and I were glad we were there."

"Me too," Gibson said quietly. "It made things easier. Thanks."

"Always, sport, you know that." Jack's tone grew aggrieved. "The flight home the day after was shit though. We hit some damn thunderstorm and the plane was shaking side to side like a rag doll in a terrier's mouth. Beth was petrified, and I have to say I needed new knickers too."

Gibson snickered. Jack wasn't fond of flying. "Aww, diddums. You big baby. It was a bit of turbulence."

"Turbulence?" Jack's voice rose. "I was thrown about like a damn piece of ice in a cocktail shaker. I don't know how Maxwell does it all the time."

Gibson snorted. "He told me once about this time a passenger had an epileptic fit in the middle of a huge storm, and there was some old woman who kept standing up and telling everyone the world was ending and they were all going to die. She was trying to drive the devil out of the poor guy jerking in the aisle. They had to forcibly restrain her and belt her into another seat with an air steward holding onto her while they dealt with it all. The other passengers were getting pretty scared."

Jack gasped. "Oh hell, that sounds awful. I guess you need your wits about you to manage that sort of thing. Maxwell strikes me as someone who's pretty put together though."

Gibson smiled. *Unless he has a bad hair day.* "Yeah, he's a rock. I'm sitting waiting for him to get home."

There was a grin in Jack's voice when he spoke. "No doubt you're going to jump his bones the minute he walks in the door? I smelt the cologne in your room. It was your getting laid one."

Gibson sniffed haughtily. "Are you referring to my Paco Rabanne *Invictus*? Any man would want to bone another one after smelling it."

Jack cackled. "Sorry, not me. I'm immune to your charms. Now give me a lady dressed in *Paris* and I could say the same thing. I love the scent."

Gibson groaned. He knew Jack sprung a hard-on for the fragrance. He'd been with him last Christmas when they'd trawled every department store in the world looking for the right perfume to buy Beth. *Paris* had eventually made the grade.

Jack chuckled. "Anyway, let me go and let you get it on with your man. I assume this means you won't be home tonight?"

Gibson nodded smugly. "You assume correctly. It's been a while and if I don't have sex tonight, my balls will explode and paint the walls."

There was silence on the other side. "Nice…thanks for sharing that image."

Gibson giggled and was mortified at the sound. He never giggled. "Pleasure. Oh and when I get home tomorrow we can have a catch up on where we are with the game and speak to Emmett and the others. I'm done my side but it will be good to have a pow-wow. I know I've been a bit distracted lately."

"You got it. And stop beating yourself up about not being around. We'll get *Camp Queen* finished in time, I promise. See you tomorrow, Gib. Say hello to Maxwell for me."

Jack rang off and Gibson put the phone down in a spare space on one of the crowded side tables. He'd managed to get Max to start packing some stuff away but some areas he didn't like to see touched. This side table was one. It currently held an old lamp, shining refracted light through a crinkled lamp shade, a battered copy of the book *Moby Dick*, a leather belt rolled into a ball, a tarnished silver chain with a grinning skull, which Gibson knew had been Levi's, and an old gold locket containing pictures of Max's family—his mum, dad and brother. Max wore the silver chain sometimes, normally when he went out but not at work.

Max had gone into a total panic one time when the jewellery items had disappeared. Gibson still felt guilty about putting them away in the side drawer thinking the small items would be safer there and hadn't wanted to tell Max what he'd done. When he'd had the chance, he'd retrieved the items and placed them on the floor under the sofa. When he'd *found* them triumphantly a few minutes later, he'd thought Max was going to cry with relief. Since then, this table stayed strictly untouched. It was obvious these things held great personal value.

He sat, texting Cruz to find out what was new. He and Craig were still travelling somewhere in South America, currently on a private island, having the time of their lives and it looked like they'd be there for a while still. Gibson was happy for his friend but he missed his vibrant personality and warm hugs. And when he heard the front door open nearly two hours later, after the over indulgence of some Ferrero Rochers and a half a pint of strawberry cider he'd found in the kitchen, Gibson was more than ready to welcome Max home. He was tired of watching endless episodes of *CSI*, which was all there was on the television worth watching as Max didn't have

Sky, Now TV or Netflix. Max was frugal with his money, not surprising given his past.

Gibson launched himself into Max's arms as he came into the lounge. Gibson wrapped his legs around Max, latched onto his neck and proceeded to kiss him to death. Max appeared startled at first but soon got into the mood and before long, they were both panting, gasping messes on the couch, half dressed and more than ready to take it further.

"This is some welcome," Max managed to get out in between evading Gibson's tongue. "Did ya miss me then?"

Gibson sunk his teeth into Max's throat, eliciting a cry of pain. "Can't you tell? Plus I'm high on chocolate and cider—never a good combination."

"Oh I think I like this combination," Max gasped as he fumbled with Gibson's jeans. "I can't say the same about this damn zipper though."

Gibson flung himself back on the couch as he unzipped and pushed his jeans down his legs. He smiled slyly at the heat appearing in Max's eyes and the sultry gaze down at his groin. Soon Gibson was naked apart from the clingy white thong he wore.

"You…" Max's voice choked up. "I can't believe you're wearing that."

Gibson frowned. "Why, don't you like it?"

Max was having trouble breathing. "Oh I like it very much. I had this fantasy of you a while ago in a white Speedo, coming out the pool all wet, and I could see everything…and here you are now, dressed in that. It's a dream come true."

"Not quite true," Gibson smirked. He leapt up and went to the kitchen. Taking a large bottle of water from the fridge—not too cold as the fridge didn't work well—he unscrewed the cap and took a long swig of water, letting it dribble down his chin onto his bare chest. Max's dark eyes stared at him in lust.

Gibson gave the bottle to Max and lay back on the couch. "First, you get your clothes off," Gibson murmured. "Then you pour this all over me, right here…" He palmed his cock and groin suggestively and a frisson of delight sprinkled his skin like a warm breeze at the look of greed on Max's face.

"God," Max said faintly as he stood up and divested himself of all his clothes. "You are such a fucking tease." His brow furrowed.

"Shouldn't we put a towel or something down though, so the couch doesn't get too wet? I mean we have to sleep on it tonight."

Gibson made an impatient gesture. "God, babe, whatever. Wet me so you can fuck me please. I'm dying here." Trust his anal-retentive partner—he sniggered—to think about something clean-freaky at a time like this.

Max scowled and went over to the sideboard. He opened the door and took out a spare towel then came back. "Lift up," he instructed. Gibson rolled his eyes but did what he was told. Once the towel was down, Max knelt before him with the open bottle and leaned in.

"And for the record, I'm not *fucking* you," he whispered.

Gibson's mouth opened in an indignant protest—hadn't they been here before, what was wrong with the man?—but was muffled by the soft press of lips against his.

Max released his mouth, leaned back and positioned the water above Gibson. "I'm making *love* to you."

The first drops of water fell onto Gibson's groin and he took in a breath. The water was cool, thank God, or his cock might have shrivelled to nothing. Although from the intense expression on Max's face, the quickening of his breath and the dilation of his pupils, Gibson had a feeling he'd have no problem getting to full mast again. And when Max filled his mouth with water and leaned down to douse it on Gibson's cock at the same time he mouthed it through the wet fabric, Gibson knew he'd have no problem sustaining his erection. God, he could come from this sensuous water play alone.

By the time Max had wet him with both his mouth and by pouring from the bottle, until Gibson's front was soaked and his cock and balls pushed pinkly through the delicate white fabric, Gibson's hole was aching to be filled and possessed by something other than the fingers currently pressing insistently inside him.

Max was hard, his cock bobbing as he leaned in and out, delivering this particular form of water torture. The look of rapture on his face turned Gibson on like nothing else. He was being worshipped and adored, and it was a heady feeling.

"You look so damn sexy lying there. My very own wet dream." Max poured what was left in the bottle onto Gibson's cock and then sat back, gazing at him with eyes drinking him into their depths.

"Please," Gibson mewled. "I need more than your fingers inside me."

Max opened a condom and sheathed himself. "Do you ever want to reverse things more?" he asked huskily as his fingers ran trails through the wetness on Gibson's belly. "Because you know if you do, that's fine with me. I don't mind either."

"I thought you liked topping?" Gibson said; the thought of making love to Max was appealing. Gibson was a bottom at heart, but with Max, he enjoyed being inside him.

"I do. But for you, I'd do anything and enjoy it. You know that, baby."

Gibson considered then shook his head. "Not tonight. Tonight I want *you* to take *me*. I want to do you again, but not tonight."

Max chuckled sexily. "That's more than all right with me." He finished dripping the rest of the water lazily onto Gibson's stomach and chest, leaning down and lapping the moisture pooling in his belly button.

Gibson moaned. "I'm ready to fucking explode here and I want to do that with you filling me up. Stop teasing."

Max grinned and took Gibson's mouth in a cool, wet kiss as he fulfilled Gibson's basest desire and slid into him. Eyes the colour of autumn leaves stared into his intently as between them, they fulfilled each other's need for one another. Gibson closed his eyes and fell into the sensation of being owned, of being seduced and being…loved.

Slow, steady thrusts of Max's hips, coupled with his own needy movements to meet the slick skin of his lover's groin, made Gibson smile dreamily as his fingers gripped firm buttocks and urged Max deeper.

There was no need for words. Soft sighs and groans were the only sounds permeating the dark recesses of the room and Gibson moaned softly as his climax built. He managed to groan out a word.

"Fuck…" He shuddered as he came, warm streams of sticky come coating them both as his arse clenched tighter. Max gave a strangled groan and murmured Gibson's name. His body stiffened and he gave one last, slow push of his hips then he buried his face in Gibson's neck. Teeth nipped the sensitive skin of Gibson's throat and he let out a small cry of pain and satisfaction.

"Are you eating me, Max? 'Cos that's what it feels like."

Max lifted his head, hooded eyes filled with emotion staring down into his. "I want to bloody consume you," he whispered as he moved away. "Any way I can. God, honey. You turn me into an animal."

Gibson nodded in drowsy satisfaction. "Hooray me." He reached out a languid hand. "Now give me those damn wet wipes and let me clean myself off. I'm all sticky and I want to curl up beside you and go to sleep."

Max handed him the ever-present wipes and they cleaned themselves up and then crawled under the duvet. Gibson snuggled into Max's right side and gave a contented sigh.

"I missed you so much and this is the best way to spend the night. I love being with you."

"Me too," Max said softly against his hair. "I wish I could have been there for you when you had the funeral."

Gibson trailed fingers across Max's damp, wipe-fragranced stomach. "It was fine, lover. Stop beating yourself up about it. You're here now. *You're all that matters.*" He closed his eyes and burrowed deeper into the duvet and Max's body.

Max gave a soft sigh and pressed a kiss against the top of his head. "I'm glad you feel that way. I was going to tell you about this tomorrow but I think now is the right time." Max shifted and Gibson heard him take a deep breath. "I'm transferring to ground crew in a few weeks. I got the job."

At first, it didn't register. Gibson heard the words 'transfer' and 'ground crew' in his head and satiated as he was with sexual release, he didn't quite process it. Once the penny dropped and he realised what Max had said, he shot upright, covers falling from his body.

"What? When did this all happen?"

Max shrugged and turned on his side to face him. "I had my interview a while ago and they decided I was a good fit their team. While I'll be working different shifts, night and day, at least I won't be on stay-overs and flying around the country. I'll be home more often." His voice faltered. "Is that okay? I mean, I thought you'd be pleased, because you always say you don't see me enough..."

The vulnerability in that voice made Gibson's chest ache. "Of course it's okay with me. You know that. But are you sure? I mean you loved flying, and I'd hate to take that away from you."

"I love you more," Max blurted and Gibson lost his breath. He stared down at Max, not quite sure what to say. They looked at each other and then Max sighed.

"Sorry, I didn't mean to make you uncomfortable." He lay back, throwing his arm across his eyes. "It slipped out. Fuck."

Gibson lay back too, hands clasped under his head as he contemplated the ceiling and the enormity of the words he'd heard. Had wanted to hear. They weren't unexpected—after all Maxwell had told him so before—but hearing them in the warmth of the bed they'd made love in without a fever in sight was a little scary. Another emotion warmed him too, though: joy.

"Say something." Max's voice was tight. "Anything."

"I'm thinking," Gibson countered. "I want to say the right thing."

"If you have to think about it, then maybe there's nothing to say." Max muttered huffily.

Gibson sat up and glared at Max, a surge of affection making his words less critical. "Stop being such a douche." He pulled off the covers and watched as Max removed his arm and watched him from narrowed eyes. Slowly, Gibson leaned over and traced the outline of Max's tattoo with his tongue. In between teasing licks, he carried on his conversation.

"You know, it's not the first time you've told me that." Max stiffened and Gibson grinned as he placed soft kisses across Max's stomach. "And I'm a Cancer. We like to think about things before blurting them out, not like you Scorpios who say whatever's on your mind, whenever." His eyes widened. "Oh my God, I realised you're a Scorpio and have a scorpion tattoo? How radical is that?" He could almost see Max's eyes roll at those words. "Is that why you chose a scorpion?" Gibson asked curiously.

Max growled. "No. And what do you mean you've heard those words before?" Gibson noted with delight Max made no move to stop the slow exploration of his body.

"Well, when you were sick, and I was looking after you, you told me then. Of course you thought you were talking to Dream Gibson at the time…" He bit the flesh on Max's stomach and he let out a yelp.

"I knew it." Max sat up, and Gibson moved back. "I knew there was something you were hiding afterwards. Why didn't you say anything? And what exactly *did* I say?"

Gibson smirked. "You told me not to tell Real Gibson. That you didn't want to scare me away. And look, lo and behold. I'm still here."

"So you are." Max's voice was thoughtful. "Did I let any other gems of wisdom loose while I was feverish and my boyfriend was taking advantage of the situation?" His voice was more relaxed and a little teasing. The tension had disappeared from Max's body as Gibson nibbled his ear and nodded.

"Uh-huh. You told me you liked to dress up in a furry suit and pretend to be a squirrel. Oh and I think the words 'sucking my nuts' was mentioned a couple of times..." He shrieked as Max pushed him back onto the bed, a slow smile forming on his face.

"You lying little rotter. I said no such thing." Max growled. Gibson had poked the bear now and a merciless tickling ensued, leaving Gibson gasping for breath and giggling uncontrollably. He was particularly susceptible to having his ribs tickled.

Soon, he was breathless, lying beneath Max's hard body—in every sense of the word—staring up into his face. It was a definite *moment*.

In the stillness of the room there was only each other, and Gibson could hear the steady beat of his own heart. His arms were pinned above his head as Max lay across him. He was waiting for something. Gibson didn't want to disappoint him.

"You love me, then?" he breathed and watched in delight as Max's eyes dilated and his nostrils flared. The answer, when it came, was simple.

"You know I do."

"Oh, okay. I guess it's a good thing I love you back then." Gibson reached up and encircled his Max's neck with strong arms, drawing him in for kiss. Max made a small sound and then Gibson was lost in the slippery warmth of the eager tongue in his mouth, the hands running through his hair and the insistent press of a hard body against his. When they finally drew apart for breath, both men were panting and, if Gibson's body was anything to go by, both were once again very turned on.

However, this wasn't about making love right now. It was about sharing, about the future.

"You're the best thing to ever happen to me," Gibson said softly as he rested his head on Max's chest. "I never thought I'd see it, but you enchanted me the minute you did that whole *Karate Kid* thing in the club. I didn't realise it then."

Max laughed. "You sound like someone from a cheesy romance novel." He reached over and moved a damp tendril of hair from Gibson's cheek. "I fell for you the minute I saw you on the plane."

Gibson groaned mock theatrically. "Oh, God, listen to us. Please tell me we aren't always going to be this damn soppy. I think I might throw up." But his tone was teasing. And when Max disappeared under the covers and took him in his warm and eager mouth, Gibson arched his back and gladly gave in to being cherished.

Chapter 13

Maxwell sighed happily and finished licking runny ice cream off his fingers. Life had settled into some sort of normality after Gibson's return from Scotland. The last two months had been interesting to say the least.

He'd learnt Gibson had a nasty streak when interrupted too many times from his game design. Maxwell had made the mistake a few weeks ago of distracting him not once, not twice, but three times during a particularly complicated 3-D rendering 'thingy' he was doing. The subsequent potty-mouth invectives coming from lips he'd kissed not too long ago had horrified Maxwell. The broken house phone lying in pieces in the rubbish bin had borne testament to Gibson's temper as he'd had hurled it at the wall. And Maxwell thought *he* was the one with the bad temper. Huh.

When he'd mentioned it to Jack one evening as they'd swapped stories about the creatively endowed but fiery virago currently in his living room on a conference call with some hairy dude called Everett, Jack had laughed loudly and sympathised. Apparently he'd been on the receiving end of Gibson's hissy fits more than once.

Maxwell had also found out said Everett was a former fuck buddy and was coming over for the Quasar Game Conference to be held in a weeks' time. He'd made a mental note to not let Chewy, as Jack had named Everett, go anywhere near his boyfriend on his own. Maxwell was planning on going to the Con too, even if the outpouring of geekiness he expected to encounter killed him. Gibson could get his geek on with the best of them, something else Maxwell had discovered.

Jack wandered in, munching on something looking like a cross between half a cow and a loaf of bread. It was the biggest burger Maxwell had ever seen, oozing mustard and tomato sauce down Jack's chin. Maxwell was always in awe of Jack's appetite and the kitchen at his and Gibson's flat was always stocked with the most amazing variety of foods and snacks.

"He still busy with Hairy Boy?" Jack took a bit bite of his burger. "They get on the phone and they talk for hours. Best settle in for the long haul, buddy."

Maxwell sighed. "Is he always like this? So intense when he gets his teeth into something?"

Jack nodded and cheerfully wiped a splodge of mustard off his lip and sucked it. "Yep. Gibson is a perfectionist when it comes to his gaming. He drives me crazy." He grinned fondly. "But he's a consummate professional and there's no one I'd rather do this whole business thing with."

Maxwell wiped his sticky fingers on his jeans. "The game is nearly finished then? Gibson was saying it'll be ready for next year, maybe a little earlier than February."

Jack's eyes shone. "Yeah. We've come along great these last couple of months." He prodded Maxwell slyly in the ribs. "Thanks to you."

"Me?" Maxwell was surprised. "What did I do?"

"You've kept him happy, Max," Jack said softly. "Taken his mind off his dad's death, looked after him and made sure he ate properly. He's lapping it up and it's the happiest I've seen him. You're good for him."

Maxwell's body flushed with happy warmth. "Oh. Thanks, that means a lot." Surely, he had never felt more content. Coming home to Gibson curled up on the sofa bed, reading or on his laptop, or coming over here to Gibson's house and being part of a close-knit circle that included Jack and Beth, whom he liked, was like being part of a family. And when they went to visit Gibson's family in Scotland, he was made to feel welcome too. It was eons away from his previous life as a travelling salesman of his sexual wares and high-flying cabin attendant.

"How's the new job going?" Jack asked with a squint. "Gibson says you're enjoying it."

Maxwell nodded. "It's great. Hard work, and sometimes the early morning shifts piss me off, but at least I'm home much more and we can organise a weekend together now, or time away. It was a good move."

"Good stuff, sport. Glad it all worked out for you." Jack glanced at his watch. "I need to go meet Beth. She's got drinks with her work colleagues and I'm meeting up with her at the pub. Tell Gibson I said goodbye and I'll be home later. If not, I'll text him."

Maxwell nodded. "Will do. Tell Beth I said hi and have a good time."

Jack grinned. "Yes, spending the evening with a bunch of dentists and dental nurses sounds like a dream come true. Hopefully Beth still has her uniform on. I love seeing her like that." He snickered dirtily.

Maxwell chuckled. "Go get 'em, Tiger. I like a man in uniform myself."

"Yummy, so do I." Gibson wandered through then, flashing a wicked smile at Maxwell. "In fact, baby, perhaps you can put on your old crew uniform and we can do a bit of role play, give Jack some ideas for what he can do with Beth?"

Jack's jaw dropped.

Gibson continued with a sultry look at Maxwell, whose trousers grew tighter with every word Gibson uttered. "I'm thinking bad-tempered passenger on a flight who needs to be given a little slapping to discipline him. Or maybe a big bad flight attendant who's in need of an attitude adjustment…" He struck a pose, pointing at Maxwell dramatically. "On your knees, boy and suck my dick!"

Jack's face was pink. Maxwell was amazed; Jack was so put together in most ways, but mention sex—especially gay sex—and he was reduced to a blushing adolescent. Maxwell took pity on the flustered Jack.

"Yeah, Gibson, I don't think that's helping. Stop teasing him."

Jack glowered at Gibson and shot a thankful glance at Maxwell. "What he said. I'm off. I'll let you know whether I come home or stay over at Beth's. See you guys later." He disappeared then returned a few seconds later with a mutter to pick up the bag he'd left in his hasty departure.

Maxwell shook his head in amusement as he watched Jack scurry out the flat. "You are such a little bitch sometimes. You live to make that man feel uncomfortable, I swear."

Gibson shrugged and bit into an apple he'd taken from the fruit bowl on the table. "He's used to it by now. He's so vanilla and shy about sex. Sometimes I like to shock him."

"You finished your conversation with Chewy early. Jack said you two would be on the phone for hours." Maxwell slumped down on the couch and Gibson sat next to him, still munching his apple.

"We got everything sewn up earlier than we thought. I'm seeing him next week at the Con anyway so we can chat then." He frowned.

"And please don't call Ev *Chewy* when you see him. He has a thing about it. He's not a fan."

Maxwell cleared his throat. "You and he had something going then?"

Gibson rolled his eyes. "We were fuck buddies, Max, nothing serious. And he knows I have a serious fellow now so this won't be another Jamie scenario, I promise." He moved to straddle Maxwell's lap and bit off another large piece of apple. His mouth approached Maxwell's and Maxwell opened obediently as Gibson fed it to him from his mouth. Gibson smiled in approval as he chewed the sweet fruit.

"Good boy," he crooned. Maxwell shuddered in anticipation as he realised what role play Gibson was acting out. He got his confirmation a minute later when Gibson lifted Maxwell's shirt over his head.

"Now, sweet slave boy, it's time to give the master his reward," Gibson whispered sultrily. As another piece of apple was pushed into his mouth, followed by a wriggle of Gibson's arse against his cock, Maxwell surrendered.

*****

Wall to wall geek. Maxwell wasn't sure what the collective noun was for a bunch of them gathered together at a gaming conference, but he thought perhaps a google of geeks might be a good term. Maybe even a nerd herd. He sniggered and Gibson looked over at him through his new thin, sexy, black-framed glasses and raised an eyebrow.

"What's so funny?" Gibson asked with a pout. His eyes darted around the venue like a fish in a bowl. He'd been on tenterhooks about today for the past week, both at seeing Everett and taking part in the convention set in the middle of London on a cold and overcast November day.

"Oh, nothing," Maxwell said airily. "Checking out the atmosphere, immersing myself in the rush of geekiness flowing towards me." He flapped a hand, feigning a swoon. "I'm feeling quite faint with it all."

Gibson scowled but his eyes smiled. "Don't be a dickhead."

He looked delectable in dark blue chinos, an open, long-sleeved white shirt with a darker blue string necktie strung loosely around his neck and a brocade waistcoat, in shades of grey and bronze. Maxwell wanted to eat him all up.

Gibson's brow creased in an adorable frown. "I'm looking for Ev; he said he'd be here by now but I haven't seen him yet..." His voice trailed off as he peered around the room.

Maxwell sighed. He'd been preparing to meet the man Jack—who'd been with them earlier but disappeared into the crowd—called Chewbacca. Gibson appeared to think of the world of Everett from Canada, and Maxwell wanted to make sure he followed suit. There was a small niggling jot of jealousy lurking in his soul but he'd manfully tried to suppress it.

"I'm sure he's around, isn't he, like seven feet tall and hairy? He should be easy to spot..." His own voice tailed off as Gibson's eyes flashed dangerously.

"You've been listening to Jack, haven't you? I'm going to kill him."

Maxwell decided wisely to keep quiet and not cast any further aspersions on Everett. He sighed and resigned himself to being dragged through the teeming crowd of men and women all talking about things Max couldn't even pronounce. He was out of his depth. He was pushed, pulled, jostled and had his feet stood on half a dozen times before Gibson gave a loud, joyful cry and let go of Maxwell to literally jump into the arms of a man standing amongst a group of earnestly gesticulating geeks.

"Ev, I've been looking for you everywhere, you bastard. It's so good to see you." Gibson's enthusiastic greeting didn't escape Maxwell and he noted sourly that 'Ev' certainly didn't seem to mind being mauled by a sexy blond dynamo. He waited patiently though until Gibson had finished hugging and kissing the man on the cheek thankfully and then turned to him, eyes sparkling.

Truth be told, Maxwell was a little disappointed. Jack had built up this picture of—well, a comical, Chewbacca type of character—and Everett Talbot, while hairy, wasn't true to the image at all. Ev was a six-foot, broad-shouldered, good-looking man of about thirty, with a thick beard, dark, thick, rusty-coloured hair and yes, hairy arms and chest that showed though his polo shirt. It resembled a safari hunter's lion trophy hanging on a wall.

He was a bear and Maxwell didn't want to think of his man and this one together because it made him way twitchy.

He smiled politely when Gibson introduced them.

"Ev, this is my boyfriend, Max. He works for London City Airport, but he used to be cabin crew. He gave it up so he could spend more time with me." He cast an adoring glance at Maxwell who basked in those words. "Max, this is my friend *Everett*." His tone held a warning and Maxwell gave a little sigh. He'd better not upset the apple cart and call the man Chewy after such an adoring look from his lover. He wanted more of them.

"Hi, Everett, great to meet you." Maxwell squawked as he held out his hand, expecting it to be shaken and instead found himself with a mouthful of burly chest as Everett hugged him like the proverbial bear.

"Hey, Maxwell, great to meet you at last. I've heard so much about you from this little tyke I feel I know you already." Everett's voice echoed in Maxwell's ear as he tried to extricate himself from the vice grip he was encompassed in. Finally breaking free and running a hand over his hair to make sure it was okay, Maxwell nodded.

"Oh, he's talked about me to you?" His natural sense of smugness lurked close to the surface as he considered the import of those words. "What did he say?"

Everett laughed, a loud belly laugh, and everyone turned around to stare at him, despite the hub of the arena. "God, he doesn't stop. It's Max this, Max that. I can't wait for Max to get home so I can bone him, yada, yada, yada."

"Really...?" Max drawled, watching Gibson's face go pink. "How interesting..."

"Yeah, enough bromancing and spilling my secrets, you big hairy bastard." Gibson punched Everett on the arm but it was like a gnat swatting—well, a bear. Maxwell was still affronted at the fact Gibson got to call Ev something hairy when he'd been warned off it.

Gibson became all bossy, something Maxwell loved to watch. "We've got some stuff to talk about, Ev, so maybe we can grab a coffee and find a spot at Coffee Dork, and you can tell me about those improvements you made to the program."

"Coffee Dork? That's a real place?" Maxwell said faintly. He was overloaded with nerd-dom and it was starting to hurt. He liked playing games as much as the next man but this was too much.

"It's a proper franchise, Max," Gibson said with a long, suffering roll of his eyes. "I'm gonna take Ev over there, we'll have a quick talk and I'll come and find you later. Maybe we can meet in a couple of hours over there by the giant locust thingie. I think it's supposed be Locula, the vampire locust from *Green Scream*." He waved towards a ceiling-high green monstrosity in one corner with waving antenna and what looked like a sound booth on its back. People were actually climbing rope ladders to get up to it. Maxwell looked at the vampire locust then back at Gibson who stood there, tapping his foot impatiently.

"You call a couple of hours a quick conversation?" Maxwell said in dismay and pique. What the hell was he supposed to do for two hours on his own?

Jack appeared beside him as if by magic, cackled and shoved him in the back. "I told you they talk for ages when they get together. Come on buddy, I'll look after you. I'll find you something to occupy your time. Gib, Chew—" Jack bit off the word as Gibson stared daggers at him. "Ev, see you both later."

Maxwell didn't even have time to say goodbye before he was hauled for time immemorial through the seething mass of humanity. He finally finished up somewhere he knew he'd like and he wanted to kiss Jack for introducing it to him. The bar was called Pablo's. Maxwell heaved a sigh of relief when he and Jack found a spare table and chairs and sat down. It was lunchtime after all and Maxwell could do with a beer. Jack winked and went off to order them as Maxwell sat back with a sigh and took out his mobile. He might as well catch up on the world of Twitter and Facebook while he was here.

Three beers and two and a half hours later, and there was still no sign of Gibson. Maxwell was feeling a little woozy and he needed fresh air. Jack had been a consummate host, keeping him company in between visiting certain exhibits—obviously, he wasn't as big on this exhibition as Gibson was—but Maxwell needed some space. And peace and quiet. The constant chatter and noise in the hall was fraying his sanity.

"I'm going to go outside, get some air," Maxwell said to Jack as he stood up.

Jack nodded. "Cool. I'll tell Gibson where you are when he gets back. I'm going to stay here and try get to the next level of this game." He looked up. "It's probably raining. You might need an umbrella."

"*If* he gets back," Maxwell muttered. "And I don't have a brolly." Thoughts of him and Everett had been flitting through his mind, and while he trusted Gibson, his insecurity was bleeding through.

"He'll be back," Jack said confidently. "Stop being such a worry wart. He gets a bit distracted."

"Okay. Well, let him know where I am and I'll hopefully see him in a bit, not too wet." Maxwell picked up his jacket, drained his beer and stopped to take a pee on his way out. After a veritable mission getting to the entrance, he finally made his way out into the overcast, drizzling climes of the city.

"Great," he grumbled. "Bloody raining again." It had in all truth only been raining for two days, which by British standards wasn't bad, but he was in a bit of a mood. He'd known Gibson had things to do, but he was missing him. And the fact Everett had *his* Gibson wasn't making it any better.

"Oh grow up, you stupid git," he told himself as he stood, shivering with the cold breeze despite his thick, wool-lined denim jacket. "Stop being such a misery guts." Scolding himself for his stupidity made him feel a little better.

He took a few deep breaths of the rain-scented air as he watched the denizens of the capital walking past in Macintoshes and coats, huddled underneath umbrellas. His eyes noticed a figure huddled in a shop front two doors down and his heart sank. One thing Maxwell couldn't do was resist giving something to the homeless people who lined the streets. It was the least he could do. He usually gave food, coffee or warm clothing but he had none of those things at the moment and nowhere to buy them. It would have to be money.

He opened his wallet, took out two five-pound notes and walked over to the figure sitting in the corner, hidden by a blanket already spattered with rain. He squatted down in front of them, not too close, knowing from experience sudden moves could startle some of the street kids. That alone could cause all manner of mayhem, perhaps even a knife in the ribs.

He'd been there and done it himself before, threatened someone with a sharpened skiv he'd made from a plastic knife taken from a McDonald's. The well-meaning man had taken him by surprise after he'd had to fight off a john who hadn't wanted to pay for the blowjob he'd given him in the alley. Maxwell had already suffered a black eye and a kick to the nuts as a result of that escapade and he hadn't wanted any more abuse. Needless to say, the well-wisher had beat a hasty retreat, but he had left the sandwich he'd bought behind.

"Hey," Maxwell said softly.

The figure stirred and muttered and Maxwell crinkled the pound notes in his hand. "I don't want to leave this here. I'd like to make sure it gets put somewhere safe. Can I slip it under your sleeping bag cover?" Levi had hated anyone touching any of his stuff and had a tendency to become a little violent when he thought someone was trying to take something away from him.

The figure mumbled something and lifted the cover away from the face. Maxwell saw an old woman with pale, grey, stringy hair and dulled blue eyes. Her face was weathered, the familiar signs of crack and alcohol abuse staining her features.

Maxwell knew people looked at the homeless and thought all they'd do was go buy drugs and booze with the money they'd been given. But even drug addicts needed food and warm clothes, and when he and Levi had been together, the money had been spent in equal parts in putting food in their bellies and finding shelter. Maxwell had refused to use it to keep Levi in drugs. That had been money Levi had to find himself. It had been a catch-22, and one Maxwell had battled every day. Until the day he'd woken up and discovered he no longer had to worry about Levi.

"You can give it to me," the woman said hoarsely and Maxwell pressed the money into her grimy hand. Her eyes squinted at him and he stood up, not expecting a thank you. He turned to go back to the shelter of the game venue.

"Mooch?"

His body went stiff, and it wasn't with the cold air blowing down the street. His throat closed up and the blood rush to his head made him feel faint. He swung around slowly and faced the woman who had the gleam of recognition in her eyes and a slight smile on her face.

"It is you. I'd know those brown eyes and chin anywhere." She shook off her blanket and stumbled to her feet. "Don't you recognise me? It's LouLou."

Maxwell's teenage past came flooding back in a cacophony of memories, both wanted and unwanted. LouLou had been one of Levi's dealers. She and Levi had had a special bond that went beyond the simple supply and demand relationship. The pair had been like family, with Levi going to her when he'd had words with Maxwell, or wanted to be alone.

Three weeks before Levi had died, LouLou had disappeared and Levi had got agitated about it. She'd never shown up again, and Maxwell thought she'd simply moved on—or worse, died and been carted away. Levi had gone back to their old meeting place, a shop corner in the dregs of town, but he'd never found her again. Levi had been truly devastated by her loss. Until the day he died, when he'd come back from meeting another one of his dealers, and he'd appeared a little more upbeat. Maxwell had never found out why, despite his prodding and then—well, then it had been too late. Levi had died and Maxwell was left alone.

"LouLou. Of course I remember you." Maxwell was shocked. Eleven years ago she'd been a woman who admittedly looked rough but a lot better than she did now. The years and no doubt the drug abuse had taken its toll on her body to the point he hadn't recognised her.

She nodded eagerly. "You look so different, so grown up. You got off the streets then?"

Maxwell nodded. "Yes, I managed to move on when Levi died. You remember Levi?"

Her eyes slid away from his and she nodded jerkily as she stared at the ground. "Of course, he was a good lad. I was so sorry he died. I told him not to, but he still did." The words made no sense.

Maxwell frowned. "Told him not to what?"

She looked at him then her gaze faltered again. "He found me. I'd been away, in a shelter. I'd been sick. But he came looking for me for his stuff, and I gave him some. But it wasn't good." Her drug-addled brain was no doubt confused but the chill down Maxwell's spine grew colder.

"Wait—are you telling me you gave Levi the shit that killed him that night?" The freezing chill was no doubt melting now from the burning anger stabbing his gut.

When she opened her mouth and the words spewed forth it was as if she was unburdening her soul and Maxwell was her avenging angel.

"He'd always trusted me. And I told him it wasn't good stuff, that I got it from someone I didn't trust. But he said he needed it and I let him take it. I needed the money. He said he'd chance it." She slumped against the wall, her face twisted in guilt. "I never meant to kill him. When I heard the news I knew I'd have to disappear for a while, in case the cops came looking for me." She wailed in despair. "I'm sorry, Mooch. He was a good lad. I know you loved him. He loved you something fierce, he did."

Maxwell could barely focus with the remembered grief and the heat of rage threatening to immolate him. "You fucking bitch." His venomous tone made her shrink back in fear, clutching the wall. "He trusted you and you fucking murdered him."

He heard his suppressed street roots growing like greedy grasping tendrils through his mind and body. "He vomited to death and I found him cold and lifeless. Because of you and your bad shit he put in his veins, I was left alone!"

LouLou shook her head in panic. "I'm sorry, lad. I didn't mean to hurt him." She cowered against the wall.

"Max." Gibson's voice echoed in the dull throbbing of Maxwell's mind. "Baby, calm down. She's an old lady, you're scaring her."

Maxwell snarled as he swung round. "I'd never hurt her, Gibson. That's not who I am. You need to back off though. This is my business, not yours."

Oh, God, listen to me. I've turned back into Mooch. I can't be him. I can't.

Gibson's face was pale, his glasses speckled with rain, his slight form shivering in the cold. "Anything upsetting you is my business, Max." His face was grim but determined and Maxwell had never loved him more. But this moment wasn't about love. This moment was about hate and despair and rage at every shitty thing he'd ever been forced to do to survive, brought back by the sight of a woman on a pavement, the woman cowering before him.

"Leave this alone. She killed Levi, for God's sake!" Maxwell spat.

Gibson stepped forward, his face filled with compassion and love. "I heard what she said. I didn't want to interrupt, because I thought you needed this. To find out what happened all those years ago. But it's not going to bring him back. Levi has gone, Max. But you still have me. I'll help you through this." He stepped forward, arms open as if to take Maxwell into them, and Maxwell lost it.

He shoved Gibson away violently, needing space, wanting nothing more than to run, to get away. Gibson cried out but Maxwell needed solitude, somewhere to lick old wounds suddenly torn open. He turned, feet pounding the wet pavement as he escaped. He wanted to be anywhere other than back there, in that moment.

Maxwell wasn't as fit as he used to be, and his breath came in heaving gasps as he pushed and shoved his way through the people going places. It was only when he stopped for breath and spied an alleyway, with a large dumpster in it, and a plethora of cardboard boxes, that he finally stopped running and slumped down onto the cardboard, back against the wall, as he fingered the silver chain around his neck. Levi's chain.

Gibson's face swam in his vision and he clung to that loving visage as he sat in the cold alleyway until everything went dark and he remembered no more.

Chapter 14

I'm fine. Leave me alone for a bit. Don't come over. I'll call you soon. I'm sorry about everything. So damn sorry.

Gibson sat on his couch, curled into the corner as he huddled under his duvet. He'd stared at the text countless times in the last two days. It was the last message he'd had from Max since he'd ran off into the darkness, leaving Gibson with a scared, guilt-ridden homeless woman and a nasty, deep gash on his temple and a swollen right eye where he'd hit the wall after Max had shoved him.

Jack had been incandescent with rage when he came to his friend's aid after his panicked phone call. Max had been called every name under the sun as Jack had taken Gibson to the first aid room to have his wound dressed. Jack had thought he needed stitches but Gibson had firmly disagreed. He hadn't wanted any more fuss made.

His chest ached both from seeing his lover's pain and at being rejected. He'd had to spill the beans on Max's past to Jack to explain why he'd lost it, and while sympathetic to Max's grief and past history, Jack had growled angrily there was no excuse. Gibson had agreed, but he'd quietly argued with Jack it had been accidental.

He knew deep in his bones that Max would never hurt him on purpose.

LouLou had packed up her bundle of meagre belongings and scarpered. Gibson had watched her go through blurry streams of blood running into his eyes and a headache of note. His glasses had also been damaged in the meeting with the wall, and they'd now been resigned to the bin.

Gibson had wallowed in his own misery the past few days. Jack and Beth had been there for him, insisting on staying every minute with him to ensure he didn't have a concussion.

Gibson knew Jack had texted Max with a terse, uncomplimentary message about how he'd hurt Gibson and he was a complete dick. Max had replied then, as Gibson's previous texts had gone unanswered.

He stared morosely into the depths of the couch, seeing nothing and wondering how things had gone so terribly wrong that night. He'd gone outside searching for Max only to find him shaking with temper and looking very un-Max like. The soft, sweet, funny man

Gibson knew and loved had turned into a tough, feral ruffian intent on hurt. Mooch was back. Gibson had heard the conversation, and his stomach had gripped with dread. He'd had to intervene.

"Not that I helped the situation at all," he murmured now to himself. He sighed and reached over for his sketchpad. He'd had little appetite to work on *Camp Queen*, which was nearly complete. He had a few minor touch-ups to do before they sent it their beta testers. Instead he'd started idly drawing his and Max's story in graphic form as a means of staying close and reliving their relationship.

He smiled softly at the images before him in his white drawing pad. They were black and white pencil renderings of Max's famous crane kick in the club; Gibson falling over the fence, hurting his hand and Max with his handkerchief, kissing it better. There was even the scene with the heaped clothes on the bed while Gibson sobbed in Max's arms on the floor.

A soft touch on his shoulder made him look up. Beth stood there, holding out a cup of tea. "Here, drink this." She handed the mug to him and he nodded his thanks. She sat down beside him and her eyes widened.

"Wow, these are incredible," she breathed as she looked at the drawings. "You are so damn talented. I wish I could draw like you."

"Yeah, well I might not have the real thing but I have this." Gibson traced a picture of Max lightly with his finger. "I wish he'd come over so we can talk, you know? I don't know what's going on in his mind anymore."

"Sweetie, he's hurting too, I know he is. That man adores you. It's on his face every time he looks at you. Yes, he's being an arsehole, but he discovered something that threw him for a loop." She sighed. "It didn't give him the right to do what he did and not talk to you now, but I think he'll come around. Be patient."

She flipped the sketchpad and her face softened at the picture of Max sitting beneath a tree with Gibson seated between his legs, leaning back against his chest. "That's beautiful," she murmured. "You two look so good together. That's how I know things are going to be okay."

Gibson stared at the picture wistfully. "We went to Sherwood Forest for the weekend and pretended we were Robin Hood and his Merry Man. It was a great weekend."

Beth sat up, her eyes brightening. "Gibson, why don't you make this into a comic? If Maxwell sees these pictures, he'll have to know you love him. It'll remind him of all the good times. Maybe it will bring him to his stupid senses."

Gibson raised his eyebrows. "Seriously?"

Beth smiled. "I'll take it over and drop it off for you because I guess you don't want to go to his place yet." She grimaced. "Don't ask Jack to do it. He's so mad with Maxwell, he'll probably punch him."

Gibson considered the suggestion. The more he thought about it, the more he liked the idea. Max couldn't possibly ignore the fact they were important to each other if he saw these pictures. He grinned at Beth, feeling hopeful. "I'll do it," he said decisively. "I have all the software already to make the storyboard, and the right paper, and my hot shot printer-scanner. I'm sure I can make some sort of a graphic comic out of all this. Great idea, Beth."

Half a day later he still hadn't heard from Max, but Gibson had a beautiful colour comic ready to go, and he put it in an envelope with a brief note he hoped wasn't too soppy.

Wanted you to have this to remind you of our time together. Please talk to me. I love you.

Beth left him with a soft kiss to his forehead and a promise to deliver it to Max's door. And if he wasn't in, then she'd leave it in his mailbox.

A day later Gibson was ready to climb the walls. Beth had assured him she'd left the envelope in his letterbox, yet Max still hadn't called him. Now Gibson sat in the dark, again under his treasured duvet, the soft strains of classical gaming music playing on the sound dock on the sideboard and wondered if it was finally over. He'd even called Max to ask him if he got his comic. Nothing. It had gone straight to voice mail. Texts remained unanswered.

Gibson hadn't been sleeping. He'd cried himself to sleep more than once, and he was beginning to doubt he'd ever hear from Max again.

Beth and Jack had gone out an hour ago to a film première and Gibson was alone. He fingered the healing scar on his temple and winced. It was still livid and tender, and his eye was a little swollen with some yellow bruising. He reached across to the side table and picked up his well- worn copy of the extra comic he'd made for himself. It was an unhealthy obsession, flicking through the pages, reminding himself of past events.

He'd done some further work on *Camp Queen* but his heart wasn't in it. That irked him; his passion for something had been relegated to an activity he did because he had to. Max had replaced Gibson's love for his art and it both thrilled and frustrated him. He was a lover first and an artist second now. He hadn't even told his mother or brother yet about Max not speaking to him. If his mother thought he was heartbroken she'd never give up bugging him, especially so soon after his father's death.

There was a soft knock on the door. His heart leapt but he daren't hope. After all, it could simply be the neighbour who kept coming around asking for all manner of things to borrow—a screwdriver, a cup of ice, a triple-A battery. Gibson pushed the duvet off and padded to the door in his socks. His dress sense lately ran to warm tee shirts and baggy sweatpants and he didn't care what he looked like right now. Cruz would have a hissy fit at the current state of affairs. But Cruz was now in Rio de Janeiro with Craig, living the good life.

He slipped the safety chain on in case a serial killer stood outside then opened the door. He lost his breath.

Max stood there, hair mussed and curly, dark shadows under eyes, which were dull and lifeless. His face was pinched, his usual cheery demeanour lacking, but it was the hesitancy and wariness in those brown eyes that made Gibson want to cry. Max looked as if he never expected anything good to happen to him ever again.

"Max." Gibson closed the door briefly and took off the chain. When he opened it again, Max's eyes were drawn to the bruise around his eye and he paled, visibly upset.

"God, your face. I never meant to hurt you—please believe me. I got scared and pushed you away, but I didn't do it to hurt you."

"I know it was an accident," Gibson said quietly. He gestured inside. "Do you want to come in?"

Max nodded and hitched his rucksack tighter onto his shoulder. Gibson stood aside as Max entered, then closed the door and padded back into the lounge, sitting down on the couch and drawing his duvet around him like a safety blanket.

Max stared around the room nervously, then sat down in the easy chair, his rucksack on his lap. His fingers fidgeted with the straps.

"Jack's not here," Gibson said tiredly. "He and Beth went out. You're not going to get beaten up. I wouldn't let him touch you anyway."

"That's more than I deserve," Max said quietly.

"Bullshit," snapped Gibson angrily. "Where the hell have you been? Wallowing in self-pity? It hasn't been a picnic for me either, you know."

Max sagged down in the chair and closed his eyes as he passed a hand over his hair. "I know. God help me, I know. Jack told me what I'd done to you, your beautiful face and I was ashamed. I couldn't bring myself to face you."

Gibson snorted. "And you thought by ignoring me it would make things better?"

There was silence.

"I hated myself for losing control like that," Max said finally. "It took me back to the time I was on the streets, trying to stay alive and out of trouble." He laughed harshly. "I thought it was all behind me until I saw LouLou again. Finding out it was her who gave Levi the drugs sparked something inside and I lost it." He gulped. "And I hurt you too. I—" he took a deep shuddering breath, the anguish on his face breaking Gibson's heart. "I hurt the one person that means the most to me."

Gibson closed his eyes briefly, his throat clenching as the ache in his chest magnified. "I'm not so sure about that." He shifted and clutched the duvet. "I can't compete with a dead man, Max. I can't. I know it was a long time ago but you have these memories I can't replace and I doubt I ever will."

Max stared at him wide eyed. "What?" He put his rucksack down on the floor and knelt down in front of Gibson, as if in supplication. "Baby, you aren't competition for Levi. You never were. There is no comparison. I never loved Levi like I do you." He raised his hands helplessly. "I realised something these past few days. Levi and I only had each other. We protected one other, looked out for each other. It was a relationship born of necessity. I loved him and I always will. But it wasn't like what I have with you."

"What do you mean?" Gibson asked, hope flaring in his chest that perhaps things weren't too late to be fixed.

"I mean I have this amazing guy, this clever, funny, sexy man who makes me feel indestructible, who loves me for everything I am and never judges. I have this man who makes me feel like I'm the most special person in the world, and I fucked it up. And do you know what he still did?"

Gibson waited, not sure what he was supposed to say. Max reached inside his bag and brought out a now tattered copy of the comic.

"He made me this. He drew all the places we'd been, all the things we'd done, good and bad, and he sent it to me with a note saying he loved me." Max's eyes shone with tears and Gibson was ready to bawl too. "It was the singular most incredible moment of my life when I saw this gift and knew he still loved me despite me being a prick. I cried for a whole day, every time I saw it. I even took it to bed with me because I couldn't bear being parted from it. It made me feel close to you."

"I thought you didn't like it," Gibson whispered. "It took you so long to get here."

Max reached up and cupped his face in shaking hands. "I needed to pull myself together so I could come here tonight and tell you this. I needed a little time to get my head straight." His voice choked up. "I love you so much, baby. I thought I'd lost you." He stood up and motioned to Gibson to lift the duvet. He sat down next to him and pulled it back over them both.

"I thought I'd failed Levi when he died. I'd always looked out for him, kept him safe, even though he was the older one. Finding out I couldn't have saved him—it hurt. These past few days I realised he died because of the drugs he took, not because I let him down. The feelings I have for you are more than anything I felt for him. You are my world, Gibson Henry, and I'm going to spend my time proving it to you, if you'll still have me."

He leaned in and removed Gibson's glasses, laying them gently on the side table. He kissed Gibson's swollen eye, then the ugly gash on his temple. "Battle scars *I* put there," he murmured sadly. "I'm so sorry. What can I do to make it up to you?"

Gibson stared into those brown eyes he loved, falling into their depths, and whispered, "Kiss me, you idiot. It's been ages."

The words had hardly left his lips when he was pushed back against the couch arm and Max's mouth found his. He'd expected frantic, frenzied kissing born of need but instead found himself subjected to a tender and loving embrace as Max worshipped his mouth. Halfway through the kiss, Gibson felt wetness on Max's cheek and opened his eyes to see a solitary tear trickling down Max's face. His heart stuttered, tightening with emotion, and he pulled away and softly traced the stain on Max's skin.

"It's okay, Max. We're fine, I promise."

Max nodded and slid his hands beneath Gibson's baggy tee shirt. "Take me to bed, Gibson." He gave a watery smile. "I'd hate Jack to come home and find us naked together, it'll blow his mind. And I don't need any excuse for him to kick me out."

Gibson chuckled softly. "Yeah, that would drive him over the edge. And he won't be kicking you out. Come on then." He pushed Max away and struggled to his feet, dragging the duvet off and trailing it behind him as he walked to the bedroom. He switched on the light and threw a stray red shirt over the top to create a sexy ambience. It didn't take him long throw the cover back on the bed and start undressing. Luckily his room was toasty warm thanks to the central heating. Max followed him and stood in the doorway.

Gibson looked at him as he took his glasses off, then his shirt and plonked it on the chair. "You okay?"

Max stared at him from shadowed eyes. "I want you to undress me."

Gibson's body thrummed with delight. *That* thought sent a rush of blood to his dick. In the past, Max had always ripped his own clothes off in haste and the thought of slowly disrobing the man in front of him was heady.

"Sounds good to me." He pushed his trousers off his hips and stepped out of his briefs, leaving him nude and evidently ready for action. Max looked at his groin and licked his lips. The little movement sent Gibson into a tailspin.

"Christ, Max, stop looking at me like that," he said breathily. "You're going to make me come."

"Not before you take off my clothes and make love to me," Max murmured softly. "Make me yours completely. I need this."

Gibson walked over to him as Max regarded him with eyes shaded chocolate with desire, biting his bottom lip.

There was no need for words as Gibson lovingly, gently disrobed Max. First to go was the polo shirt. Max lifted his arms and blew out a soft exhalation of breath as the shirt was pulled over his head. Gibson sucked on the rosy nipples left bare and smiled around them at Max's moan.

Next, while still sucking on the needy buds of flesh, Gibson unzipped Max's jeans and pushed them down over his hips. Gibson teasingly caressed the erection beneath the silk of Max's boxers.

"God, Gibson, you are killing me." Max's body was tense, his hands wrapped around Gibson's waist.

Gibson ignored him, simply went down on his knees and mouthed the thick cock he found, revelling in his lover's hiss of need. The silk fabric was spotted with wetness and Gibson took great delight in slowly sliding them down Max's legs to fall in a whispery heap on the floor.

Max's cock sprung up, and Gibson hummed a happy sound as he took it in. Max gave a stifled cry and grasped Gibson's head, winding his fingers through his hair. Gibson had no problem being pushed down or further onto what he had in his mouth. He rather enjoyed it, loved the rough treatment and a man fucking his mouth. Especially if that man was Max.

"Not too much," Max gasped. "Want to come when you're inside me, not like this."

Gibson finished licking a long swathe up the outside of Maxwell's dick then looked up. "You want me to fuck you?"

"No," Max said, sounding a bit irritated. "I want you to make love to me. I need to be yours completely tonight."

Gibson's own cock perked up. "Get onto the bed." Gibson kissed the tip of Max's prick and stood up, going over to the side table to take out condoms and lube. Max moved onto the bed and watched as Gibson bounded onto the mattress and slid in beside him.

Gibson waved the lube mischievously. "I guess lube is your friend, then? It's been a while since I've been in you."

Maxwell nodded, eyes heated. His fingers closed around Gibson's cock, squeezing it and Gibson let out a squeak.

"Shut up and do this." Max lay back and widened his legs in invitation.

Gibson didn't need further urging. He picked up the lube, opened the tube and dribbled it onto his fingers. He covered Max's body with his own, finding his lips, and as they ravaged each other's mouths, he slid slick fingers inside Max. He loved the fact he had a squirming, moaning man underneath him as he opened him up, making sure to find the spot inside that made his man buck beneath him and cry out.

And when the time came to slide inside Max, cock sheathed and gasping at the perfect fit of them together, Gibson was ready. Max's hoarse entreaties to go deeper, to move, to take him spurred him on to obedience and soon there was nothing but the perfect rhythm of two men moving together.

Sweat, wet, heated skin, scented musk and fevered kisses was all it took for Gibson to reach his peak and explode inside the hot, tight channel of his lover. Max's strong legs were wrapped around Gibson's waist as Max stared up at Gibson with swollen lips and hooded eyes. Max pumped his own cock a few times and then he too was climaxing in a spill of sticky essence, coating their bellies and chests.

Gibson slumped on top of Max with a groan. "Oh, God, that was incredible. We are *so* doing that again soon. I don't know why I don't do it more." He slid off to lie beside Max on the bed, as he tried to draw a breath. He plucked the filled condom off his dick, tied a knot in it then placed it on the bedside table. Normally he'd throw spent ones on the ground but if Max stood on it in the middle of the night, he'd never hear the end of it.

Max was quiet and Gibson turned, propping himself up on one elbow, and gazed at him. "Are you okay?"

Max reached up and caressed his jawline. "Awesome. That was amazeballs."

Gibson cackled. "Amazeballs? Now who's the geek?"

Max grinned. "There's no doubt about who's the geek in this relationship, lover. You wear that badge with honour and pride." He sat up and kissed Gibson's eye gently, then the healing scar on the side of his face. "Thank you for not kicking me to the curb."

"Now why would I do that?" Gibson murmured as he snuggled into Max's side. "I love you. People in love forgive each other. What's a little smack against a wall between friends?"

Max winced and Gibson backpedalled. "That was a joke. Bad taste, sorry."

They lay in silence for a while then Max shifted. "I need to clean this stuff off before it itches. Where's your wipes?"

Gibson huffed. "In the bathroom. God, you are such a neat freak."

Max sniffed as he got out of bed. "Forgive me for not wanting to stick to the sheets."

He padded naked to the door and opened it. It was with a sense of surprise when Gibson heard a loud shout of "Oh, for fuck's sake put some damn clothes on!" as Max came scurrying back into the bedroom and slammed the door.

Max stood stock still in the room, face scarlet, as laughter welled in Gibson.

"Jack came home early, huh?" Gibson sniggered and then the floodgates released and before he knew it, he was rolling on the bed howling with mirth. Tears rolled down his cheeks as Max stared at him indignantly.

"Fuck, he saw me in the altogether, and so did Beth," Max sputtered as he quickly pulled on his sweatpants. "I thought they'd gone out?"

"So did I," Gibson managed to get out in between laughter. "Something must have gone wrong. Oh, God, your face, you looked like a rabbit running from a fox."

"You are such a little bitch," Max huffed. "How am I supposed to go out there now? Not to mention Jack wants to kill me."

Gibson finally managed to stop laughing, but held his aching sides as he got out of bed. He peered around myopically for his pants and slid them on. "I'll go find out what's going on, shall I? You can sit here and cower in bed, you big sissy."

He nimbly sidestepped a slap to his behind and opened the door to escape into the hallway. Jack's bedroom light was on and he knocked on the door then barged in. "I thought you two were out for the night? Sorry you got an eyeful of Max's junk, but *I'm* rather partial to it."

Jack's face was scarlet as he sat beside Beth, who was pale and lying on Jack's bed. "Beth got one of her migraines so I brought her home." He flashed an ill-tempered stare at Gibson. "What's he doing here?" He flushed. "I mean, I can guess what you were doing but are you two an item again?"

Gibson pursed his lips. "Yes, we're all good now. He was looking for the wipes to clean himself up when he ran into you."

Beth sniggered. Jack looked uncomfortable.

"Oh joy. TMI, Gib," he muttered as he gently brushed hair off Beth's cheek. "Are you saying I can't give him a good kick now for what he did to you?"

Beth slapped Jack on the arm. "That's exactly what it means, you big bully." She smiled wanly at Gibson. "I'm glad you got back together. That makes me happy." Her face went a little green and Gibson was concerned at the pallor of her face. "Jack, I think I'm going to be sick. Could you get me the rubbish bin because I don't think I'll make it to the bathroom?"

Jack was up in a flash and handing her the small wastepaper bin. She retched and leaned into it, obscuring her face. Jack held her long hair away from her face.

"What can I do?" Gibson asked feeling useless. "Can I make tea or something?"

Jack shook his head. "Nah, she needs to get it all up and then lie down in a dark room." He cast a fond glance at Beth. "I'll be with her, we'll be fine. You go back to your naked antics." He scowled. "And tell Maxwell from me if he hurts you again all bets are off."

"Yes, dear," Gibson said snarkily. "Do you want me to tell him he's grounded too? Or put him on the naughty step? His face grew thoughtful. "I rather like the idea of grounding him on the naughty step...or should that be grinding?"

He chuckled at Jack's death stare and blew a kiss at Beth. "Hope you feel better, my lovely. I'll see you both in the morning. I have a scaredy-cat fella to go harass. Nighty night."

Beth laughed softly. "By the way, Gibson? Max *does* have nice junk."

Jack glared at her as Gibson sniggered and left the two alone.

He remembered to stop by the bathroom on his way and fetch the wipes.

Chapter 15

Maxwell leaned back in the posh chair he sat on around a beautifully dressed table filled with chatting, enthusiastic people. He and Gibson were in Manchester for the weekend at what Gibson jokingly called the 'semi-prestigious' gaming award event called the British Gaymz Choice Awards. Gibson had told him smugly it was *the event* for the design and production of LGBT games—and where gay gamers gathered. He'd subsequently sniggered at the clever use of alliteration.

Maxwell had no idea there was actually a gay gaming community, and Gibson had seriously informed him sometimes it became tiresome to trawl beneath the anti-gay slurs in some other forums. Years ago, an LGBT group decided in order to have their technical questions answered, and converse with like-minded individuals, having their own forum was the way to go. The best reason for Maxwell currently sitting surrounded by a bunch of people talking about things he couldn't hope to understand, was that *Camp Queen* had been nominated in one of the categories; Most Anticipated Game of 2016.

Maxwell had been loftily informed that the online forums talked amongst themselves and held a vote on what game they were looking forward to. Gibson and Jack's game was on the list. Maxwell had known Anomaly Media was popular and their games were well received, but finding out Gibson and Jack were two of the hottest properties in the gaming community had floored Maxwell. Both men played it down with a sense of humbleness.

Maxwell watched as Gibson leaned over to the man sitting next to him and laughed at something he said. Maxwell couldn't hear much—the noise level was deafening—so he smiled and stared around him. He'd never been one for big events like this, where the cutlery shone under bright lights, huge bouquets of flowers festooned the table and everyone wore a monkey suit. It was all exceptionally Christmassy, with only one week to go before Christmas Day.

They were spending a few days up in Manchester after the event, visiting Canal Street, taking in a couple of shows and generally winding down from the events of the past six months.

Things had been getting better between them every day and Maxwell thanked whatever mythical gaming gods lived above that he still had Gibson in his life.

He cast an appraising glance at Gibson who looked edibly sexy tonight in his tuxedo with its Chinese lapels, a black and white polka-dot bowtie wrapped around a crisp, white shirt, which moulded to his toned body. Maxwell was looking forward to peeling it off later tonight in the hotel.

He wriggled uncomfortably in his new suit, and cursed the slow creep of his briefs under the tight trousers. Gibson had taken him shopping and insisted this one fitted perfectly, but Maxwell was finding it a little constrictive. He had seen the appreciative gleam in Gibson's eyes when he'd come out of the bedroom suitably attired. Maxwell had the smug feeling he'd be getting lucky tonight.

Gibson turned to him and winked, placing a warm hand on his. "Okay, Max?"

Maxwell huffed. "You mean apart from not understanding a word anyone is saying and having my knickers trying to eat my arse? Oh yes, I'm cool." He grinned as Gibson chuckled.

Gibson moved closer and lowered his voice, staring at Maxwell over the top of his spectacles. It was an action that never failed to turn Maxwell on; it was such a sultry move. Especially when it was accompanied with a lick of pink, ripe lips. "You tell those knickers it's my arse to eat and I fully intend doing that later."

Maxwell's trousers grew even tighter and he gulped. "Bitch. You've made me spring a hard-on."

Gibson's sultry laugh again made Maxwell's cock swell. He opened his mouth to no doubt say something equally as saucy when the microphone on the stage echoed and the compère, some famous gaming multi-millionaire called Alex de Clair, cleared his throat.

"Ladies and gentlemen, your attention please. I trust you've all enjoyed the delicious food, got yourselves a drink or two and enjoyed the evening so far. We're ready to begin the ceremony now so please make sure mobile phones and tablets and the like are switched off, or muted, so we can respect the entrants and the wonderful presentations we're about to see. A huge amount of hard work has gone into the evening, and the nominees deserve our full attention. Thank you."

The lights dimmed as everyone sat back to enjoy the show. Jack and Beth slipped in to their seats beside them; they'd been at another table talking to someone they knew.

"Here goes nothing," Jack said, as he loosened his bow tie. "No matter what happens, short shit, we did good. We're going to rock with this game next year."

"I know we will." Gibson shot him a fond glance as they fist bumped. "I'm nervous though."

Beth reached over and placed her hands on both Jack and Gibson's arms. "You two are champs," she murmured softly. "My heroes."

The performance began. Maxwell had to admit it was worthy of being classed in the same category as the Royal Variety Performance. There were famous musicians performing, actors he'd seen in some of the movie blockbusters, and various scantily clad men and women dancing on stage. It was professional and entertaining, and when a well-known comedian came on stage, Maxwell laughed until tears ran down his face.

And, of course, in between were the things they'd come to see—the gaming community's games of the future. Maxwell was bowled over by the quality and attention to detail in them, and marvelled at the creativity involved. He stole a glance at an enraptured Gibson, whose eyes shone as he watched the fruits of his peers' labours.

When *Camp Queen* was shown as a nominee, and there were snippets of the game on the enormous screens on stage, Maxwell could find no words. He'd seen bits of it on Gibson's laptop, and been privy to some of the detail in the game. Seeing it in full screen in public with everyone ooh-ing and aah-ing and realising this was Gibson's work—and Jack's too of course, and poxy Everett, but in his mind mostly Gibson's creation—stunned Maxwell into silence. Tears pricked his eyes at the sheer scope of the game and he blinked them away furiously, dabbing surreptitiously at them with his pristine, starched napkin.

Maxwell loved his comic book with a passion because Gibson had made it especially for him. Yet this game unfolding before his eyes was simply more proof his lover was a genius. He'd never been so proud of him. Later he had a special gift of his own for Gibson for Christmas. Maxwell warmed thinking of what lay in his shoulder bag.

He held Gibson's hand tightly as he smiled softly at him, and they watched the category nominees finish. He closed his eyes and prayed for probably the first time in his life to a god he didn't believe in, as well as every other fate he knew, for Gibson to win.

When the introduction was over, Gibson's tightening of hands alerted Maxwell he was as nervous as he was. Beth whispered to Jack soft words of support and encouragement.

"You're amazing and I love you," Maxwell whispered to Gibson. "No matter what happens, to me you won hands down."

Gibson smiled, his eyes a little teary at those words and he nodded. "Thanks, baby."

There was the usual anticipation before Alex de Clair opened the envelope and kept the audience waiting.

"It seems we have a winner," he said in his lilting Irish tone. "I have to say I probably agree with this decision, even though I'm not supposed to take sides. But I've been watching this little company go from strength to strength and marvelling at the attention to detail and amazing game play produced by them. They are truly a force to be reckoned with in the gaming world, and I see big things ahead for them." He paused dramatically.

Gibson squirmed beside him. "For fuck's sake get on with it," he muttered as Jack nodded his agreement. "Tell us already."

"And the winner is…" There was another pregnant pause and Gibson squawked again in protest. "Anomaly Media for *Camp Queen!*"

Beth's shriek made Maxwell's ears bleed but he didn't care. All he cared about was looking at the stunned expression on Gibson's face at the fact their game had won Most Anticipated Game of 2016.

"Oh my God," his lover said faintly as he sat there, gob smacked. Jack was equally as blindsided. "We won?"

"Yes, honey, you won." Maxwell punched Gibson in the shoulder. "Now go and up there and get your award."

Beth was pushing Jack out of his seat too, and both of them watched as Gibson and Jack made their way to the stage. They both looked shell-shocked.

"Oh, God, Maxwell, isn't this awesome?" Beth said dreamily as she gazed after them. "It's a dream come true for them both to win an award like this."

Maxwell nodded and clasped her hand as they watched their respective partners ascend the stage and stand beside Alex. There was some conversation between them and hugs as the award was handed over. Jack looked uncomfortable being in the spotlight and pushed Gibson forward to accept it.

Alex grinned at their obvious discomposure. "Congratulations guys for this achievement. I meant what I said. I've had my eye on you boys for a while and this is a real achievement for you both. You should be very proud. I'll be talking to you both about your future plans."

He handed the microphone over to Gibson, who took it wildly and glanced out at the audience. He pushed his glasses up with his index finger, and Maxwell smiled at that familiar gesture.

"Uhmm, this is a huge surprise. I mean, a *huge* surprise." His voice tailed off and Maxwell wanted to run up and stand beside him, tell him to milk this opportunity because he so deserved it. "I think I speak for both myself and Jack when I say we are absolutely honoured and thrilled to have won. I'm not used to giving speeches so I hope I don't say the wrong thing, but there are so many people to thank, I'd be here all night if I did." There was an appreciative chuckle from the audience. Jack fidgeted beside Gibson, looking as if he wished he was anywhere but the stage.

Beth giggled. "He looks so gormless up there. He hates this sort of attention. But oh my, he's my man and I am so damn proud of him."

"I hear you, sister," Maxwell murmured. "Our men are awesome."

Gibson found his second wind. "The guys I want to thank know who they are, and believe me, I'll be contacting each and every one of them after this show to tell them how grateful I am to have them as colleagues on this project. Jack"—he turned to his friend who was pink cheeked at being singled out—"Jack has been the best business partner and collaborator ever and he deserves a round of applause." The room exploded with clapping as poor Jack blushed scarlet and mumbled something. Maxwell thought ruefully Beth's hands were going to catch fire at the rate she was clapping.

The room grew quieter and Gibson stood further towards the front of the stage. "There is one special person I want to thank out there. Someone who held me together and gave me the encouragement and support and love I needed to get through some tough times."

Maxwell closed his eyes briefly. Surely Gibson wasn't going to…

"His name is Max, and he's my boyfriend. He's been there for me and now that I have an audience, I'm going to take the opportunity to tell him how much he means to me. Max, baby, I love you. Thanks for helping us make this happen." He held up the award to a fierce round of cat calls, hoots and more clapping. Maxwell's heart swelled so much with love he thought he might burst.

"He's killing me here," he muttered and Beth laughed and punched his arm.

"That was so sweet," she said dreamily. "He is so romantic."

Gibson turned and said something to Jack, who scowled fiercely and shook his head. Gibson muttered something. Jack capitulated and took the microphone, looking ill at ease. Beside Maxwell, Beth drew a breath and leaned forward expectantly.

"Uh, yeah, I'd like to thank everyone too, what he said." Jack jerked a thumb at a grinning Gibson. "And also tell my girlfriend Beth I love her too and she's the best thing that ever happened to me." He hurriedly passed the microphone back to Alex.

Beth was sniffling now, and Maxwell passed her his napkin.

"Ladies and gentleman, another round of applause for Gibson Henry and Jack Cunningham from Anomaly Media!" Alex de Clair beamed at the audience as Gibson and Jack exited the stage.

Maxwell couldn't wait to congratulate Gibson in a more intimate and up-close–and-personal way, but he supposed he'd better stick to a hug and a kiss for now.

Maxwell stood up as Gibson reached the table and pulled him into his arms. He held him tightly, nuzzling his soft hair. "Thanks for what you said up there," he said, half choking on emotion.

Gibson pulled back and kissed him softly. "I meant every word," he murmured, his eyes shining. "You're my rock, Max. I never thought I'd say that to anyone." He held up the award. "This means a lot to me, but you? You're everything."

The next kiss they shared was not as gentle and Maxwell vaguely heard cat calls and whistles from the crowd as he was thoroughly mauled. He wasn't complaining though. When Gibson finally released him, Maxwell was dazed. Jack and Beth beamed beside them.

Jack spoke excitedly. "Did you hear what Alex de Claire said up there? He wants to talk us about the future. What do you think it means?" he asked excitedly.

Gibson shrugged. "Not sure, but it sounds like we have some fun times ahead."

Maxwell reached into his bag. "I have something for you too," he stammered to Gibson. "I was going to give you this later but now seems the right time." He pulled out a crumpled pile of A4 paper, tied into a roll with bright red, green and white ribbons, with a multi-coloured glitter bow perched on one side.

Gibson stared at the present. "This looks interesting," he murmured as he took it and began unravelling the strands. Maxwell confessed wryly to himself he may have gone to town a bit on the ribbons.

Once the wrapping had been relegated to a pile of colour on the table, Gibson rolled the sheet open.

"What the hell is it?" Jack peered over Gibson's shoulder curiously, Beth beside him. Maxwell saw Gibson's eyes widen and grow bright as he looked up at Maxwell.

Gibson grinned, the joy in his eyes hard to miss. "The perfect end to a perfect evening," he announced.

He laid the sheet down on the table. It was a copy of Maxwell's *Sexcella* Worksheet, set with a smiling picture of Gibson in the middle and '*Stuff #5, he's my #10*' written in one corner of the photo. There was another comment at the top of the document: 'TO BE DELETED–NO FURTHER USE' written in big black letters.

Gibson looked gob smacked. "Max, you're crazy, you know that?" His eyes were filled with love. "This is such an awesome present, thank you."

"I still don't get it," Jack grumbled, squinting at the sheet. "I mean what the...oh. Shit, Maxwell, you kept *this* sort of detail?"

His face screwed up in embarrassment and Beth giggled. "Sweetheart, you'll need to bleach your eyes if you read any more."

Gibson drew Maxwell into a deep, passionate clinch and for the moment, Maxwell heard and saw nothing more. When Gibson released him, Maxwell was rock hard and ready to roll.

"Not fair," he squawked, making sure his dinner jacket still covered his groin. "We need to go home right now."

Gibson laughed. "Later. Right now, I want to celebrate with you, catch a dance or two on the floor and then we're going to back to the hotel so I can bonk your brains out." He winked and Maxwell's groin grew hotter. He liked the idea.

The sound of Frankie Goes to Hollywood's 'Relax' blared into the room and Maxwell grabbed Gibson's hand to drag him onto the dance floor. As they gyrated to one of his favourite tunes, and he watched Gibson's blond hair fall into his eyes, his spectacles steam up, and his beloved face crease in a smile as they stared into each other's eyes, Maxwell knew he'd got exactly what he wanted for Christmas.

The End

AUTHOR NOTE

Last winter, when I worked in London, I tried to give my coat to a homeless man who was barefoot in the snow and had only a thin jersey around his shoulders. He was in his sixties (or maybe younger; we all know living on the street ages people) and he shook his head.

"Madam," he said, "you're a woman. I can't take your coat. I'm a gentleman."

He took the coffee I bought him and walked down the street, still barefoot, before I could give him anything else. That sense of pride and dignity has stayed with me.

Those people on the street once had a family, a life. They have a story to tell, and there but for the grace of God go I.

ABOUT THE AUTHOR

Susan Mac Nicol is a self-confessed bookaholic, an avid watcher of videos of sexy pole-dancing men, a self-confessed geek and nerd, and in love with her Smartphone. This little treasure is called 'the boyfriend' by her longsuffering husband, who says if it vibrated there'd be no need for him. Susan hasn't had the heart to tell him there's an app for that.

A lover of walks in the forest, theatre productions, dabbling her toes in the cold North Sea and the vibrant city of London where you can experience all four seasons in a day, she is a hater of pantomime (please don't tar and feather her), duplicitous people, bigotry and self-righteous idiots. She likes to think of herself as a 'half full' kind of gal, although sometimes that philosophy is sorely tested.

In an ideal world, Susan Mac Nicol would be Queen of England and banish all the bad people to the Never Never Lands of Wherever-Who Cares. As that's not going to happen, she contents herself with writing her HEA stories and pretending that, just for a little while, good things happen to good people.

Boroughs
Publishing Group

Did you enjoy this book? Drop us a line and say so! We love to hear from readers, and so do our authors. To connect, visit www.boroughspublishinggroup.com online, send comments directly to info@boroughspublishinggroup.com, or friend us on Facebook and Twitter. And be sure to check back regularly for contests and new releases in your favorite subgenres of romance!

Are you an aspiring writer? Check out www.boroughspublishinggroup.com/submit and see if we can help you make your dreams come true.

Printed in Great Britain
by Amazon